RISING FATE

WOLF MOON ACADEMY TRILOGY

JEN L. GREY

CHAPTER ONE

My heart pounded in my ears, and my long dark hair stuck to the nape of my neck. I hated that Evan was making Sherry and me fight one another even if it was for training. Not even a week had passed since the Los Angeles alpha captured her after she had tried escaping his pack. She had been beaten and in so much pain then; it was hard for me to want to fight her now.

"She's healed now, so you're on equal ground." The Eastern heir was strong and deadly. He was the epitome of intimidation. He was huge with light skin, gray eyes that sometimes appeared white, and short, spiky, auburn hair. His tank top clung to his body molding to his muscles, and he somehow made the Wolf Moon Academy logo sexy. When I had first met him, I thought his muscles were bigger than his brain, but I was learning more and more that I had been wrong. "Even if she wasn't, there is no time to coddle everyone anymore. We all know what's going to be coming soon."

Sherry and I looked at one another, and she nodded her head as if telling me it was okay.

"Fight now," Evan growled as he watched Sherry and I circle one another on the mat.

I held my hands up in front of me. I had stupid boxing gloves on them as if it was going to make the blows not hurt. "She was hurt badly less than a week ago." It didn't feel right sparring with her even though all signs of her attack were gone. Her jade eyes sparkled and nearly matched the emerald in mine instead of appearing lifeless like they had before. Her long blonde hair was pulled back into a ponytail. Sherry was almost my height, and her hands were down at her sides as she waited for us to begin. We'd saved her from being forced into a mate bond with the heartless Los Angeles alpha.

"So were you." Evan stepped onto the mat and glared at the both of us. "After what we've seen the past week, it's more important than ever that you learn how to fight and survive. Do you not want to be able to protect yourself?"

He knew I did. I'd been kidnapped, forced to see my brother chained to a tree, and attacked by some shifters while trying to save Sherry.

"Of course I do." I took a deep breath and met Sherry's eyes. "Are you ready?"

"Yeah, let's do this." She stood in a fighter's stance and got ready to attack. "I don't ever want to be put into a situation like the one you found me in ever again, and I need to kick ass for the rebellion."

That was a point of contention Bree had confided in Sherry and she was determined to be part of it with us. At first, I was worried, but she was convinced that no one should ever live the way her pack did.

"First, let's do some standard punches and blocks." Evan's voice returned to normal as he saw we were ready to move.

In an attempt to avoid another lecture, I closed the distance between us and pulled my right hand back, aiming for her face. Just as my arm surged forward, Sherry lifted her arm, blocking the punch.

"Good. Now more," Evan commanded.

We circled around one another on the blood-red floor mat as if we were dancing. Once again, I attacked, keeping my eyes on her face but, this time, aiming for her stomach. She raised her hands, ready to protect her face, while I struck hard right into her abdomen.

She stumbled back a few feet and wrapped an arm over her waist. "Dammit," she groaned.

"Good," Evan nodded at me. "Only bad or arrogant fighters will let you know where they're going to strike. You have to watch their body movements and read them. Their eyes can flicker to your face while they target something else. Body movement is the only real indicator of their intention. Now, again."

This time, Sherry attacked, and I was able to block her hit. However, she kicked her leg out, aiming directly at my chest.

I stumbled backward but managed to barely block it with my arms. "Hey, he said practice blocking and punching."

"Do you think it's going to be a fair fight when you're fighting for your life?" Evan arched an eyebrow. "Mia, you know better than that."

He was right. I did.

My eyes landed back on her, and she raised her hands in front of her once more.

She wasn't hesitating, so neither should I. I tapped into my wolf and ran toward her. I stared directly into her eyes as I threw a punch. She was able to block it, and when I went to kick my leg out toward her, she spun around, placed her arm around my neck, and hit my still injured shoulder. Dammit ... it still hurt, but I didn't want anyone to know.

Taking a deep breath, I did the only thing I knew to do. I leaned over, causing Sherry's body to fly over my own and hit the mat hard. She loosened her grip around my neck, and I straddled her, pinning her body so she couldn't move.

"Good." Evan's eyes glowed in approval as I stood up and held my hand out to help Sherry up.

The air went cold as Mr. Rafferty entered the gym. "So, this is where you train them?"

Evan's body tensed as he turned around to face his father. "What are you doing here?"

"Well, after your display this past weekend, I'm thinking we should talk." Mr. Rafferty's eyes glowed brighter than normal. "You two are dismissed," he said to Sherry and me, but I refused to budge.

The last thing I wanted to do was leave Evan alone. I removed the gloves from my hands and stood next to Evan. "He's my trainer, not you."

"You are a manipulative bitch. You make them feel more important than they actually are." Mr. Rafferty wrinkled his nose in disgust. "I told Jacob it was a horrible idea to sponsor you here. After all, you're just a pack alpha's daughter, but he was intrigued by how you affected Liam. Now he regrets pushing you to come here."

It took a second for me to figure out who he was talking about. I had always thought about my mate's father as Mr. Hale, not by his first name. "I'm not the one trying to manipulate them." I should shut my mouth, but I hated how the heirs were raised. The council had killed my father, and I was going to prove it. *Liam, Mr. Rafferty is here.*

I'm not surprised. Dad has already tried cornering me today. There was a pause. *I'll be there in a second.*

"Maybe you could learn something from them." Sherry threw her own gloves on the ground and stood on my other side.

"And who are you?" Mr. Rafferty's dark gray eyes landed on her as he moved in our direction.

"I'm the new student here, Sherry." She took a deep breath, straightening her shoulders.

"So, you're the weak shifter they kidnapped from the Los Angeles alpha." Mr. Rafferty shook his head.

When we spoke to the council the other night, they'd alluded to the fact that our four-day tour of a city in each of the regions hadn't gone well. They didn't provide specifics, and we hadn't been willing to give up any information.

"Your point?" Sherry frowned at him.

He moved quickly as if he was going to attack her, and she stumbled back in surprise. He chuckled as he stared into the very apparent fear in her eyes.

"That we should hand you back over." He shook his head. "We don't need weak students here at this school."

"She's not weak, and if you hand her over, they'll know we were involved." Evan's voice was low.

"Not if we tell them we found her." Mr. Rafferty sneered at Sherry as if he was daring her to contradict him.

"I'll sing like a canary." She placed her hands on her hips and squared her shoulders at him, but her voice wavered, revealing her fear.

"They won't believe what a weakling like you would say." Mr. Rafferty's voice raised in challenge.

"If you were against an entire pack, you wouldn't come out on top either." Evan's shoulders tensed as he tried to capture his father's attention.

"Like hell I wouldn't." He took a menacing step in Evan's direction, but unlike the last time I watched his father abuse him, Evan didn't cower in fear.

"You better remember how you were raised." Mr. Rafferty's alpha will laced his words as he stared his son down. "I'm your alpha, and you will listen."

Evan kept his gaze locked on his father, but his body quivered. "You may be my alpha, but that doesn't mean I have to cower in fear of you."

"That's *exactly* what it means." Mr. Rafferty pushed his son in the chest so hard he stumbled back.

My heart broke for him even further. Evan was one of the most loyal people I'd ever met. Despite the way he was raised, he was a good man, but his father was trying to turn him into something mean, cruel, and self-involved. He was trying to turn his son into a replica of himself.

"What's going on here?" Liam entered the room, his blue eyes landing on me first. He was wearing the standard Wolf Moon Academy colors. A silver button-down shirt with the wolf howling at the moon, and blood-red slacks. He wasn't as muscular as Evan, but he could hold his own just fine. He headed over to me and stared at the council member.

"It's none of your concern." Mr. Rafferty's voice was filled with contempt as he glared at my mate. He tugged at his black suit jacket as he frowned. "I need to talk to my son alone. Why don't you take your *mate* and this weakling and leave us be?"

"No." I shook my head. There was no way I was leaving him alone with this monster.

"It's fine." Evan nodded at Liam. "I'll meet up with you shortly."

"You know where we'll be." Liam took my hand and led me toward the door.

We can't leave him like this. There was no telling what he would do to Evan. His father came in here, determined to dominate him. I hated leaving him behind. *We need to be there to prevent anything bad from happening.*

As soon as we stepped into the hallway, I stopped, waiting until Sherry had caught up to us. When she stepped out of the room and moved to stand beside me, we turned down the football stadium's long hallway that was used only by the football team and The Blood Council along with their families. It was a VIP entrance of sorts.

Mr. Rafferty is a hothead. Liam squeezed my hand in his. *In fact, it would be worse if we were there. The slightest hint of Evan not obeying would cause things to escalate with outside eyes watching them. Don't worry. He's a lot stronger than our parents know.* Liam turned left heading toward the door that took us outside. *He'll be fine.* He ran his hand down his short dark brown hair as we stepped outside.

It bothered me that I hadn't even considered that. Mr. Rafferty was the one who appeared to need control the most, which was odd since Mr. Hale was seen as their leader.

"I'd heard the council members were assholes, but for some reason, I didn't expect that," Sherry's eyes widened as she shook her head. "His dad is crazy."

"They all are." Liam sighed as he slowed our pace, now that we were out of the stadium. "It's best if you remember that."

"Have they always been that way?" I'd never asked the question before, having assumed it to be true.

"No, they weren't." Liam's shoulders sagged.

We were now walking past the woods where I'd been kidnapped only a few weeks ago. Both Liam and I were scanning the trees, looking for anything that would be suspect. Even though I couldn't prove it, the council had Amber set me up to be captured. They were trying to get rid of me after Liam had completed our bond.

"At one point in time, they were more parents than assholes." Liam shrugged his shoulders. "I'm assuming it's because we got older, but who the hell knows."

"Bree told me that they'd changed. That he treats her similarly, and she isn't even the heir to the throne." Bree was stronger than anyone gave her credit for. She may have seemed high maintenance at times, but she had a good heart and knew right from wrong.

"Maybe, but she's deemed a spare." Liam's body loosened as the girls' dorm appeared.

"I used to dream about going to this school and being around all these alphas." Sherry frowned as she glanced around the campus. "I thought it would be a place for all of us to come together and try to better our world. It's apparent that the council members are not interested in that at all."

"That's why it was initially created." Liam took in a deep breath. "Something's changed, and it didn't happen overnight."

We reached the girls' dorm, and I glanced across the large grass clearing back toward the gym and university restaurant. There was a large building far back against the tree line where the normal classes were taught; composition, algebra, chemistry, and other classes you'd find at a human university. These things should make me feel normal, but now they all appeared like looming threats. The council owned everything.

The boys' dorms were right next to the girls', which made the campus a total of four buildings and the huge-ass football stadium used for our team.

The three of us walked in the entrance of the girls' dorm

through the lounge area that was filled with couches, tables, and televisions. There weren't many students around since everyone was busy with classes. We headed to the elevators to take us to the twelfth floor.

We entered the living room area of what was technically my and Bree's dorm. Bree was sitting on the blood-red colored couch with a phone up to her ear. Her crystal blue eyes glanced up at us, and she placed a finger to her pink lips. Her long, dark brown hair, the same shade as Liam's, was pulled to the side as it cascaded down like a curtain.

"I need to grab some more clothes out of my closet and get the rest of my bathroom stuff." I'd been staying with Evan and Liam since Sherry needed a place to stay. It made sense since Liam and I were together every night.

"That's perfectly fine." Sherry smiled. "You know it's your room. I can figure something out."

"Nope, it makes sense anyway." I turned to Liam and stood on my tiptoes, brushing my lips against his. As I tried to pull away, Liam growled and circled his arms around my waist to keep me in place.

"She's not allowed to sleep away from me anymore." He deepened our kiss, making my body come alive.

"Oh, dear God." Bree hung up the phone and threw it down on the dark wood coffee table in front of the couch. "I could go forever without seeing that ever again. It's like you two are getting worse over time instead of better."

Liam pulled away slightly from me, just enough to turn his head toward his sister, and grinned. "I found my fated mate. You should be ecstatic."

"I am. But that doesn't mean I want to see you two playing tonsil hockey." Bree shook her head and looked at Sherry. "Tell them."

"Sorry, Bree." Sherry glanced at me with longing. "I hope to have that one day myself."

Simon hadn't been coming around much after things settled down. He was keeping his distance from all of us even though we all knew why. She was his mate, but the heirs had all been raised to reject their fate. It was a huge point of contention between Liam and me when I first got here. He had to work through it all on his own before he could even commit himself to the idea of a fated mate. It didn't help that Simon thought I had made Liam weak, but his tune was slowly changing.

"What's with the weird phone?" I pointed at it on the coffee table. Bree's usual cell phone had a blood-red cover with the school logo in silver. This one was all black.

"It's my rebellion phone." She grabbed the phone again and placed it in her lap.

We'd only learned recently that she had joined the rebellion while we were off, touring the four cities. During the trip, we found that packs were living in horrible conditions, working in even worse conditions, while women were being abused, and some packs even treated their members as property. When we came back, she had approached me about joining up, and that was when we stumbled onto some odd altar-type thing with the original Blood Council's logo etched into the concrete.

"Everything okay?" Sherry asked as she sat next to Bree.

Those two had hit it off, thankfully, so Bree was okay with Sherry taking over my room.

"Well, they want to meet you all," Bree said as her attention landed on me. "Tonight. It's the first step to get you integrated into the group that's been rising up against the council.

Do you think the others would be up for it? I linked with Liam as his arms dropped from my waist.

Yeah, we'll make sure it happens.

"We'll make it work." I nodded at Bree.

"Great, I'll get everything coordinated." She stood and paused as she looked at each of us in turn. "Make sure we don't regret this."

Message received. She trusted the three of us, but the other heirs, she wasn't so sure about. "We won't." I only hoped that I wasn't lying.

CHAPTER TWO

S imon breezed into his dorm and stopped in his tracks when he noticed the four of us waiting for him.

Liam and I sat on the blood-red colored couch in the center of the living room against the wall while Evan sat in the recliner on my side and Micah sat in the recliner on Liam's side. We'd already told them that the rebellion wanted to meet with us tonight, but we hadn't told Simon yet. He'd been avoiding us like the plague since the day we found the strange altar and he pledged his loyalty to the rebellion's cause. The problem was that he generally was our wild card—unpredictable. For all we knew, he'd changed his mind.

"Should I be worried?" He arched his eyebrow so high it hid behind his blond hair as his amber eyes darkened. He was slimmer than the others with a more lanky, athletic build.

"I think the question is whether we should be or not." Liam cut to the chase. It was one of his strengths in my eyes.

"Why the hell would you be asking that?" Simon's chest

puffed as he made eye contact with each of us. "I told you I was in."

"Come on, man." Micah sighed and ran his hands through his dark hair, and his golden eyes seemed to shine brighter. He was as big as Evan, but I'd been learning he wore his heart on his sleeve when it came to anyone close to him. "You've been disappearing, and our dads have been meeting with us, trying to get us to submit all over again."

"They are?" Simon's shoulders sagged with the news.

Of course, his dad knew better than to reach out to him. *Mr. Green is trying to make Simon feel excluded and playing on his weaknesses.* I'd come to realize how much he needed to feel like part of the team or he acted out on purpose.

"Why wouldn't dad come talk to me then?" He grew colder.

"Because he's mind fucking with you," Evan said with disgust. "Everyone knows you hate feeling left out or not included."

"That's not true." A frown crossed his face.

"Where have you been lately?" Liam lifted a hand. "If we don't have anything to worry about, why have you been avoiding us?"

"It's not you that I'm avoiding," Simon groaned in defeat.

It's Sherry. That's what I'd bet on, but it would be nice to hear confirmation. Neither one of them had admitted to being mates, so I was still going with my gut feeling. Also, I knew it wouldn't go well if I were the one who asked the question. Simon still didn't like me.

"Does she happen to have blonde hair and be staying with Bree?" Liam placed an arm around my shoulders as he said the words.

"What? No." His mouth dropped open and he cleared his throat. "I'm not afraid of some stupid girl."

The four of us remained silent as we all looked at him.

His face turned a slight pink, and he blew out a breath. "It's just best if I keep my distance from her. For both her and me."

"It's okay if she's your mate." As soon as the words were out, I wanted to take them back.

"Of course, you'd say that." Simon sneered at me. "You somehow coerced Liam to bond with you, but that shit won't work with me. I can't be weak."

"You think I'm weak now?" Liam chuckled.

"Yeah, you can't go anywhere without her." Simon wrinkled his nose in disgust. "I don't want to be tied down that way. You even had to take her on our tour, and we all know how that turned out. Now we're all at odds with our dads."

"First off, she hadn't planned to go with us, I wanted her there." Liam leaned back on the couch. "And secondly, if it weren't for her, we wouldn't have discovered the situation our parents have put our people in."

"Exactly. We could be blissfully ignorant, and everything would be fine," Simon said without conviction.

"Honestly, I thought the same thing." Micah stared at the coffee table in the middle of the room, avoiding our eyes. "I mean, I never thought they'd be doing that. Sometimes, ignorance is bliss."

"So you would rather people suffer so you aren't uncomfortable?" They were making this out to be more about them than what it was. "Where you can walk around with blinders on and be your dad's puppet?"

"That's not how it is," Simon growled the words.

"It's exactly how it had been." Evan touched his cheek

where the vanishing bruise was still visible. "My dad visited me today and tried to get me back in line."

"They want all of us to fall back in line without asking any questions." Liam shook his head. "Do you want to be a dumb shit following our fathers' orders like that?"

"We've been doing that our whole lives." Simon huffed. "So why would it be any different now?"

"Because we know now, man." Micah flicked his attention back at Simon. "Like I said, I thought the same thing, but it's finally becoming clear. Now, we know things, and we have to figure out what type of leaders we want to be."

"Independent from our fathers." Evan lifted his eyebrows. "If we don't figure out who we are before we even take over the council, they'll still be ruling as they always have with us following their every command."

Simon closed his eyes and grimaced. "I know, okay. It's just that I hate this coming between all of us."

"You do realize that this will bring all of you closer." I purposely left myself out of the count. I had to point out the things that made the biggest impact for him.

"How so?" He crossed his arms as he stared me down.

"You'll all be on the same side again." *You knew exactly what to say and how to make this hit home for him.* Liam chuckled inside my mind as he rubbed his fingers along my shoulder.

"I told you I was in." Simon's voice lowered as he walked over to the kitchen. He grabbed a chair and sat right in front of Liam and me.

We now made a complete circle.

"When did you get that?" Simon pointed at Evan's black eye.

"Today after training Sherry and Mia." Evan tensed.

"My dad made his appearance right before we were done for the day."

"Wait, Sherry is training with you?" Simon frowned. "She's not healed yet."

"If you'd been around, you'd know that she's pretty much back to normal." Liam shrugged.

"At this point, we all know the other shoe is about to drop. We can't afford for Mia and Sherry to be untrained and unable to stand up for themselves." Evan met my eyes with pride.

"Sherry won't be fighting in anything." Simon jumped to his feet. "She can't get harmed again."

"She's going to get harmed if she doesn't learn to defend herself." Evan waved his friend off. "So sit, and calm your ass down."

"It's only going to continue to get worse if you fight the bond." Liam sighed. "Trust me, I know."

We'd pushed him enough. Now, we needed to get to the reason we were here. We needed to leave soon anyway. "The rebellion wants to meet with us tonight."

"What?" Simon's eyes flew around the room. "We shouldn't be talking like this here."

"I checked the room twice." Micah glanced at his friend. "Besides, I'm usually the one who bugs the rooms for them, so we're good."

"That IT degree is coming in handy." Simon snorted. "When are we supposed to go?"

"Honestly, here in a few minutes, but we were waiting for you." I got to my feet. "Let's go get Bree and Sherry and then head out."

Everyone stood in agreement, and we made our way out to the area where we would meet the people we were going to start working with.

WE DROVE about an hour north of school, on the outskirts of Pittsburg, Kansas. The entire way had been an interesting ride. All seven of us had piled into Liam's Escalade, and Simon demanded to sit in the back with Sherry after Micah had volunteered.

"We should be there any second." Liam's voice grew thick with tension. The closer we got to the meeting place, the more anxiety flooded through our bond.

"I still can't believe we're meeting at an abandoned warehouse." Bree pulled her phone out again. "I mean, how much more predictable and cliché can they get?"

"How many people have you actually met from this group?" She didn't seem to know much about what's going on. She'd only been part of it for about a week now, so I guessed that made sense.

"Only a few, but I can't tell you any more than that." Bree's words were slow; deliberate.

"Will Nate be there?" Liam asked casually.

We both glanced in the rearview mirror to watch Bree's reaction.

"Is that your way of asking me if Nate is involved with them?" Bree tilted her head with a proud smile across her face.

"Maybe." Liam winced. "I mean, hell, we're going to join. Shouldn't we know who is involved?"

"You'll find out when the time is right." Bree crossed her arms.

"Dammit, Sherry, your bony elbow is poking my side," Simon grumbled as he tried to get adjusted in the back seat.

"Dude, I was going to sit there, so I don't want to hear

you complain." Micah shook his head and glanced over his shoulder. "You insisted on it, so shut up."

"I'm excited to join the rebellion." Sherry's jade eyes sparkled. "But if they are holding back information from the guys. Why didn't they from you too? You're a council member's kid just like them."

"I... I don't know." Bree's brows furrowed.

"It's because you hadn't been focused on as a council leader, not like the rest of us," Evan said as he glanced out his window.

"And the fact that your mate is part of a pack that needs some assistance." Mates had a huge influence on how we saw the world. It's how Liam and I grounded ourselves with each other. "They know your bond trumps it all."

"So that's why you kept sneaking off with that nobody loser." Simon's words were cold.

"Stop being a jackass." Sherry's voice was full of anger. "The way you're acting reminds me of the alpha who killed my father."

For once, Simon didn't have a comeback. He sat there with his mouth shut and in a tight line.

That's a first. Liam linked with me. *Maybe we should have her around all the time to keep him in check.*

Don't worry. She will be. I had a feeling that the whole thing was going to work out. They just had to work stuff out first like Liam and I did.

We entered a section of town that appeared run down. Liam's anxiety started to feed my own. All we knew was that the rebellion was forming due to packs being mistreated, but we had no clue what their plans were or how they recruited more members. We needed to under-stand what their ultimate end game was. Did they want to overthrow the council completely or only the ones leading it currently?

Liam turned down another road leading to a huge abandoned warehouse. It appeared to be an older building with the windows broken, and a huge wooden door stood out with a chain and lock on it.

"Well, I'll be damned." Liam shook his head as he pulled into the parking lot.

"Go to the back. We don't need your car parked out here where someone can see it." Evan pointed to the side where there appeared to be a side road that would take us behind the building. "Otherwise, it'll stick out like a sore thumb and cause people to come and snoop."

"Got it." Liam drove slowly as we passed by the old brick building that looked like it was crumbling. We took the side road that backed up against a forest. As we turned toward the back, we found a large truck loading area that was used for moving whatever product they had made out the door.

"Bree, what the hell did you get us into?" Simon growled as he took in the surroundings. "If Sherry gets hurt ..."

"Don't worry about me." Sherry's body tightened. "I'll be fine."

"Let's keep it together." I glanced over my shoulder. "We need to be united right now ... all of us." I opened the car door and hopped out.

Soon, the others followed suit, and we stood still, staring at the building. The back looked as if it was in a tad bit better condition than the front. It was at least three stories tall, but it was most likely just one floor as the windows were only near the ground. It was probably due to whatever equipment was kept inside.

"How are we going to get in there?" Bree stepped next to me and examined the building. "Do we open that garage door?" She pointed at the large, heavy-looking door that probably needed a remote control to lift it.

Liam took a deep breath, and his eyes scanned the area. "It looks like we're here first. Let's check a window," Liam said as he walked over to the window to his left. He lifted the window up, but there wasn't any sound. "This has been used lately. It wasn't hard to open at all."

"Let me go in first," Evan said as he approached Liam. "Then, you and Mia come through."

"Fine." Liam nodded his head and moved out of the way.

Within a few seconds, all of us had slipped through the window and walked out onto the factory floor. Tall pieces of equipment, at least half the height of the building, took up space along one wall, but we couldn't tell what it was since it was covered with sheets. Cobwebs hung everywhere and even spanned from one sheet to the next.

It was pitch black inside without moonlight shining through the windows. Thankfully, our wolf senses could penetrate the darkness. The scent of dust was thick and strong, but it was the only one in the building.

"I thought they were meeting us here?" Evan's body was tense. "Is this some kind of joke?"

"No, this is the location they said." Bree pulled out the phone and showed the text message to Evan.

Liam grabbed my hand and pulled me into him, his body tense. "This might be a trap."

"They said..." Bree cut off as fear spread across her face.

"Let's get the fuck out of here," Simon growled as he turned to head back the way we came. As he took his first step, a metal clanging came from outside.

"Hello?" Bree yelled.

"Shhh... stop it." Evan glared at her.

Another sound of a door opening came from inside the warehouse directly behind us. I turned around but couldn't smell or see anything out of the ordinary.

All of a sudden, footsteps sounded as if they surrounded us, and a wolf howled in the distance.

My heart dropped to my stomach. We'd just walked into a trap.

CHAPTER THREE

My heart pounded in my chest. We should've known better than to be so trusting. Although Bree had made us all a little more comfortable since she felt at peace with her decision. They had to have played her too.

Whatever you do, stay next to me. Liam reached out for my hand as his eyes scanned the area.

Scents hit our noses, and whoever had come into the building with us came closer.

Another loud bang came from the side of the room as if someone else had entered and slammed a door.

"We need to get the hell out of here," Evan shouted, trying to be heard over the metal clanging.

"How?" Micah yelled. "They're out there with our car. We're at their fucking mercy."

A door slammed shut, and I spun around to see that our only exit to the front had just been cut off. We were trapped.

"I'm sorry, I had no clue." Bree's bottom lip trembled. "I didn't know."

"It's not your fault." After seeing what we'd all witnessed

this past week, it made sense we'd jump at an opportunity to make a change.

"If we run, they'll follow." Sherry touched my arm. "Sometimes, the best thing is to stay put."

"Are you fucking insane?" Simon threw his hands in the air. "We won't have a chance in hell if we don't run. I can't let anything happen to you."

"Don't worry about me." Sherry growled, "I'll take care of myself."

"Guys, cool it." The last thing we needed to do was turn on one another.

Another loud howl filled the air, causing a shiver to wrack my body, and then silence. It was so quiet it was unnerving, especially after all that ruckus.

"What do we do?" Bree's voice quavered as she moved closer to me.

"They're still around us." Micah said with a breathy whisper. "It smells like hundreds."

"We're going to die." Simon paced in front of us. "See all the good you've caused. Now the council will fall because there won't be any heirs."

When I didn't think Simon could get any more dramatic, he went and outdid himself.

"Stop being an asshole," Liam warned. "We're not going down without a fight."

"It's funny that you would say that." An unfamiliar girl's voice hit our ears as the door that had been closed off opened. Her tennis shoes scuffed the cement floor as she stepped into our view. She wore a hoodie over her face and lowered her head in such a way that we could only make out her hauntingly ice blue eyes. She looked to be a few inches shorter than me, but it was hard to tell since she was at least seventy-five feet away.

"So you're going to kill us?" Liam's voice was deep, and anger was laced with each word.

"Who said anything about that?" The girl took a few steps closer to us and stopped.

"Well, it's kind of obvious." Simon countered her when growls filled the air again. "See?"

"They're only here in case something happens." Her voice sounded young; maybe around our age.

"What are you expecting to happen?" Micah asked and took a deep breath.

"She thought that we might have alerted our fathers." Evan lifted his chin in the air. "So they had to pretend that they were going to attack us to see who might show up."

The girl's eyes lit at his words. "Exactly. I mean, why would the four heirs want to join the rebellion? It seems a little suspicious."

"I, for one, wouldn't have picked this out all on my own." Simon raised his hand as if he was asking permission to speak. "All this is going to do is divide us even more."

"Divide the packs who need attention or you heirs and your relationships with your fathers?" Her voice held an edge to it and I wasn't quite sure if it was humor or anger.

"You can't be serious right now." Sherry spun around and stared at her mate. "You saw what happened to me, and you'd like to pretend you never saw it?"

"Hell, I saved you, and I'm standing right here with you," Simon came close to shouting the words. "So what's your problem?"

"Others get treated like that every day." Sherry got in Simon's space, "Does that not bother you?"

"It sucks, okay." Simon's hands shook. "It shouldn't happen, but there are assholes everywhere."

"Exactly." The girl focused on Simon. "That's why the

rebellion formed. To take down all those assholes, so my question is: Are you one?"

"He says shit without thinking it through." Micah glowered. "He's with us. He's afraid of what would happen if he wasn't."

"We're going to keep an eye on him." Her head turned in my direction. "Honestly, it's you we wanted to see."

"That figures," Simon grumbled.

"Me?" That made no sense. As far as they knew, I wasn't part of the council other than being Liam's mate.

"Yeah, we've heard about what the council has tried to do to you." She tilted her head in Liam's direction. "But you and your mate have given them a run for their money."

"It wasn't just us." I refused to take the credit. "It was a whole team effort."

"Fine. But only because we heard about what all of you did in the cities you just recently visited." She squared her shoulders at me. "This was your first test."

"Our first test?" Bree parroted the words. "But I'm already part of it."

"Yes, you are, but you're also tied to them." She gestured to the heirs. "We can't be too careful about who we trust right now. Yes, the rebellion is small, but we're growing. If we were able to truly count on the heirs to join the fight, it would make things grow exponentially faster."

"How so?" I asked. If people were feeling oppressed, why wouldn't they rally to stand?

"Because their fathers are feared, which makes recruiting harder." She raised her head, but the hood cascaded over her face. "They fear that the next in line are going to be the same way, so we're hoping to rally to catch their attention. But if you were part of the fight, people wouldn't be so hesitant since their future leaders were on the same page as them."

"In less than a year, we'll be ascending The Blood Council." Liam took a step in her direction. "So why not wait till then?"

"You guys have no clue, do you?" She shook her head and chuckled. "Your fathers are already asking the regional alphas how they would react if they stayed on for an extra year. They're citing your recent travel as evidence that you still aren't fit to lead."

"What?" Simon's voice was high pitched. "You've got to be messing with us."

"How would you know that?" Liam's brows furrowed.

"Because they have spies." Evan ran a hand over his face. "This has been going on for a lot longer than we realized, hasn't it?"

"Very smart." The girl pointed at Evan. "Not only are you strong but intuitive."

"Wait, how long has this been going on?" Micah glanced from one heir to the other.

"I've told you enough for today." The girl moved away from us. "Here's your next test. They have someone imprisoned near the school grounds. Someone important to our mission. We need you to track down where they're being held."

"How are we supposed to figure that out?" Micah asked.

"Not my problem." The girl walked backward to the door. "Once you have the info, give it to Bree. She knows how to contact us."

"If we find this, we are part of the mission too." Evan stared her down.

"That's not part of the plan," she growled.

"I guess we won't be telling you then." Liam narrowed his eyes siding with his friend.

"Ugh. Fine." She huffed.

Echoes of footsteps began moving once more.

"Wait until we're gone before leaving." She opened the door and paused before stepping through. "We'll know if you don't." Then, she disappeared.

Another howl sounded from far off, alerting all their people to leave.

"We should go out there and see how many are involved." Simon turned to leave, but Sherry grabbed his arm.

"Don't even think about it." Her tone was strong and commanding. "If you mess this up, I will take you down."

I'd expected Simon to stomp and throw a tantrum, but he remained silent.

I didn't expect that. This wasn't the Simon I knew all too well.

Neither did I. Liam took my hand and pulled me against him. *But I'll take it. Let's give them a few more minutes before we leave.*

"Does anyone have a clue where they might keep this prisoner?" Micah stared off as if he was in deep thought.

"I might know of somewhere," Evan said as he glanced at Micah. "But let's not talk about it until we're out of here. We only need to tell them what they want to know."

"That's a good premise." Micah nodded and grinned.

"What if they attack us when we're leaving?" Simon's voice raised in hysteria. "We might not make it out of here."

"If they were going to, they would've done it right away." Sherry closed her eyes. "Now, let's be quiet and listen for when they're all gone."

In only a matter of moments, the silence descended

around us once more. We slowly headed toward the window we came in through that took us back to our car. The faint scent of wolves was still there, but they were gone.

Evan climbed out through the window first, and the rest of us followed. I held my breath until we were in the Escalade and pulling out of the parking lot.

The adrenaline rush was dissipating after everything that had happened back there.

The Wolf Moon Academy entrance rose in front of us. The large black cast iron gates were open and the guard nodded at us as we pulled through the gate.

"So, are we going to talk about what happened back there?" Sherry scanned around the car. "They have to be hiding somewhere around here."

"Maybe." Evan cleared his throat. "But I'm not entirely sure yet."

"Well, let's go check it out." Bree pulled her phone from her pocket like she was going to call someone.

"No, don't tell them yet." Evan glared. "We have to make sure we give them good information and not a general hunch, or they aren't going to believe us."

"I think it's bullshit that they're trying to test us at all." Simon watched out the window from the backseat. "I mean, we're heirs, for God's sakes."

"Uh... that's exactly why." Sherry pushed him in the arm. "You act like being tied to the council is a good thing."

"Well, it is." Simon patted his chest. "We're the strongest of our kind. They should be ecstatic that we even want to meet with them."

"Dude, I don't know." Micah leaned against the car door. "I'm thinking this is more a curse than a blessing lately."

"I've got to agree with him." Liam glanced in the rearview mirror as he pulled into the dorm's parking lot. "I don't blame them for being leery of us."

"It's gotten late." Bree checked her phone. "It's after ten, and we all have classes tomorrow. Our best bet is to relax some and come up with a plan tomorrow."

"I'm down with that," Sherry said.

It wasn't long before we were all out of the car and heading back to the dorms.

AFTER CHANGING into my pajamas and getting ready for bed, I crawled in next to Liam, who was pretending to watch television.

You okay? I turned toward him and snuggled into the crook of his arm.

Tonight was a little crazy. He tucked a piece of my hair behind my ear. *For a second, I was afraid we were being attacked and I might lose you.*

Hey, I'm right here. His concern and love flowed through our mate bond. *Nothing bad happened.*

Not yet, at least. He reached over and turned the television off before moving his body toward me. *I can't handle seeing you get into situations like that. It hurts so damn much.*

It's not like I sought them out. Every situation I'd gotten into was due to The Blood Council. In all reality, they'd been interfering with my life even before I was born. *Do you think they killed my father?*

I'd love to say no. His fingers brushed his fingertips

along my arm. *But the more I see of the council's handiwork, the less I'm beginning to doubt it.*

That's what I was afraid you were going to say. I took a deep breath. *We have to help these people and find justice for my father. Are you okay with that?* It might take implicating his own father in order to achieve all of that.

I'm not thrilled about it since it proves how heartless they've all become. Liam kissed my lips. *But we will do what needs to be done for our packs and for your father.*

His lips were warm and soft against mine. I opened my mouth, enjoying his taste. We'd only been together for a month, but it felt like we'd been together for an eternity. He knew what I liked and just where to touch.

My hand traveled down his bare chest, enjoying the feel of my fingertips trailing his hardened muscle.

Damn, that feels good. He groaned, and his hand slipped slowly underneath my shirt.

As he touched me, all of the stress from the day began to melt away. In this moment, it felt like it was only him and me in the world.

He shifted so he was hovering over me and took hold of the edges of my shirt, removing it from my body. He gradually kissed down my neck toward my breasts.

I slid my hand under the waistband of his pajama bottoms and pulled them down.

He used his legs to kick them completely off of his feet while his tongue didn't miss a beat in its mission. He slipped his hands between my legs and gently rubbed.

Right when pleasure was about to wash over me, I snatched his hand and moved it away from my body. *I need you.*

Without any more encouragement, he slipped between my legs and rocked into me.

I gasped as he hit the right place inside me over and over again.

His mouth lowered to mine, and he kissed me as our bodies moved together in sync.

It wasn't long until we were both climaxing at the same time. His body shuddered as he thrust into me one last time, finishing with me.

He dropped his body next to mine and pulled me into his arms. *I love you.*

I love you too. Those words from him would never get old. It'd taken us a while to get to this point, but now it was forever.

The front door opened and then shut, bringing us back to the present. The clock read eleven at night. "What's Evan going out so late for? The restaurant is closed, so why is he leaving?"

"I bet he's going to look for the captive." Liam stiffened. "Come on, let's go. He can't do it alone. He'll get caught."

I jumped to my feet, feeling jittery. We had to stop him before something went wrong.

CHAPTER FOUR

"Dammit, he's not answering his phone," Liam said as we exited the dorm room.

"We should be able to catch up with him." We were only a minute or two behind at most. We'd thrown our clothes on as we were rushing out the door. "Let's take the stairs. Maybe we can catch up with him that way." I turned and circled the room. "Wait, where are the stairs?" I'd never taken them since we always rode the elevator.

A grin spread across Liam's face as he turned and ran down the hallway toward the stairwell. "Let's hurry."

We took the last door on the left that I'd assumed was another dorm room and ran down the stairs.

When we got to the bottom, we rushed out into the main lobby as the front doors shut after Evan's retreating back. His scent was fresh. These were some of the moments I was glad the elevators took a little while to run.

We rushed out the door after him.

"Hey," Liam called out, causing Evan to stop in his tracks.

He kept his back to us, and his shoulders deflated. "I was

hoping you got the message when I didn't answer your call."
He turned around to face us, wearing a frown on his face.

"You shouldn't go out there all by yourself." If something happened to him and we knew what he was doing, I wasn't sure if I could live with myself. "Why don't you let us tag along?"

"Because you always seem to get yourself into danger." Evan lifted a hand at me. "And if I'd asked Liam to come, you'd force us to include you."

"He does have a point." Liam jostled my shoulder.

"Doesn't matter. We are a team now." They needed to start thinking of us as friends, if not family, and not as potential competition. "I take it you're going to go check out a place."

"Yeah." Evan glanced at the moon. "It'll be better to do it now instead of during daylight hours."

"That's true, but the gates are closed." Liam motioned to the gate.

"I know, which is why it's the best time to go." Evan pointed to the woods. "I'm going to tap into my wolf and run. It's not too far away."

"Where is this place?" I didn't know the surrounding area, but the woods went on for miles.

"It's about ten miles from school." Evan waved us on. "Let's go before someone sees us out here."

He gave in fast. He didn't put up as big of a fight as I expected. He was stubborn, so it surprised me.

Because he knew that he couldn't leave without us throwing a fit. Liam winked at me.

Evan took off once we reached the woods, and I tapped into my wolf just to keep up with him. I thought we'd follow the road, but he was taking us farther into the heart of the woods.

The moon rose above our heads, and the forest was quiet except for the owls that would hoot every now and then. It was nice to run in the forest even if I wasn't on all fours. Our animal side was meant to be in nature, and we didn't embrace it nearly as much as we should between school and everything else. So these fleeting moments were peaceful.

As a gravel road came into view, Evan slowed his pace, coming to a stop. He turned in our direction as we caught up to him.

"We need to stay in the woods and follow this gravel trail," he said as he pointed down the opposite way from where it connected with a main road. "It's a good location because it's in the middle of nowhere and near a paved road that isn't traveled on all the time."

"What the hell is this place?" Liam glanced around and frowned.

"It's a secret building that the council owns." Evan grimaced.

"If that is the case, then why the hell do I not know about it?" Liam's eyes glowed as his wolf surged forward.

"Because it's only used for things that the council doesn't want anyone finding out about." Evan gestured toward the tree line again. "We need to stay hidden, but since you tagged along, I wanted you both to see this place in case something happens to me."

"Nothing is going to happen to you." If he thought we were doing a recon mission tonight, he was about to learn otherwise. "We're only here to scout it out and let the rebellion know."

"We'll see." Evan's voice was filled with determination. "I need her to know that we're on her side."

That was something strange to say. "Um... it's better if

we make sure none of us dies. What do you think would happen if one of the heirs passed away? It wouldn't be good."

"She's right. We're only here to take a look and head back." Liam straightened his shoulders. "Otherwise, I'll take matters into my own hands, and you don't want that."

"Fine." Evan's jaw clenched. "That's why I wanted to come here alone."

"I still don't understand how you know about this, but I don't." Liam frowned. "Do the other two know?"

"I don't think so." Evan shook his head as we followed the road deeper into the woods. "One night, I had to help my dad deal with a problem." His gray eyes turned to silver. "Now, I realize what he meant by that."

"Did you know who it was?" I had a feeling I knew how Mr. Rafferty dealt with problems.

"Not a clue." Evan sighed. "But that's when we didn't know to ask questions and accepted our fathers at their word. The guy kept begging for forgiveness, said he was only trying to feed his family. I'd thought he was full of shit at the time. I mean, we take care of our own."

"Or so we thought," Liam said, and regret bled through our bond.

You can't beat yourself up for that. I hated that he had moments of regret for his decisions. *You did the best you could with the knowledge at hand. If you were still making those same decisions now that you know, it'd be a different story.*

I understood that a child doesn't want to think ill of their father. We all grow up following their actions and decisions since they were our biggest influence.

"We're getting close." Evan cleared his throat, clearly not wanting to have this conversation here. "Be quiet."

"Remember, we're only going to look and not take action." I wanted to repeat that to him since he seemed determined to prove his worth to this girl. It didn't make any sense.

"Fine." He walked fast through the woods, careful not to make a sound.

We followed suit again, wondering what the hell we were going to see.

It only took a few minutes before a building came into view. It was about the size of a small apartment, and as we approached, we spotted a large, sliding glass door that was open.

I blinked my eyes once again and couldn't believe what I saw. Tripp was tied up in a chair in the center of the room. His mouth was taped over, and his blond hair was askew with his large jade eyes open wide. He was petrified.

The room was empty except for a table sitting across from Tripp, butting up against a wall, and four chairs were scattered across the room.

"Oh, come on." Amber stood in front of him, her long, straight, blonde hair was tied into a low ponytail, and her amber eyes lit with excitement. She licked the bottom of her red lips as a sickening smile filled her face. "Did you really think I wanted to date you?"

He shook his head since he obviously couldn't respond.

"Oh, fine. I love to hear you all beg." She ripped the tape from his mouth, causing him to wince.

"Ow!" Tripp opened and closed his mouth. "That hurt."

"Did you seriously expect it to feel good?" Amber giggled.

"Well, no, but damn." He opened his mouth wide one more time and closed it.

"Was that necessary?" The voice of a man I didn't recognize sounded behind Amber. "He could try to scream." The man stepped out from the shadows, followed by two other men. All three were tall and wore dark clothing with huge guns at their disposal.

"Oh, shut it." Amber turned to look at the men. "You report to me right now anyway, or do I need to call Mr. Hale to prove a point."

"No, but if he starts screaming, I'm taping his mouth back up." The man growled as he stepped outside the sliding glass door to scan the area.

I had to save Tripp. I moved when both Liam and Evan grabbed my shoulders.

If we get any closer, they're going to smell us. Liam linked to my mind. *I know he's your friend, but we have to do this smart or we'll just wind up making things worse.*

He was right. We'd just given a similar lecture to Evan earlier, but that was before I knew who it was.

"In my defense, I'm a good looking guy," Tripp nodded his head at Amber. "So why wouldn't I think that you wanted to date me?"

"You're not an heir," Amber growled the words.

"Yeah, so? None of them want to date you anyway." Tripp shrugged his shoulders as a small grin spread across his face.

"Hey." Amber pulled her hand back and smacked him across the face. "I almost had him if it wasn't for that nobody showing up out of nowhere. That's why I'm doing this. To show him how strong I am. Something that she could never be."

"Dear God, if we're going to have him talk, let's actually try something more productive." One of the other dark guards growled out. He was slightly shorter than the other two, but his face was the most angular and scary. "What were you doing hiding near the boundary in the woods the other night?"

"I told you; I wasn't spying." Tripp leaned his head forward. "I was going for a run."

"But you were hiding in the trees of the boundary line," the guard growled. "I don't believe you."

"I was chasing a squirrel." Tripp sighed. "I wasn't being lurky."

"Lurky isn't even a word," The guard snarled. "Put the damn tape back on his mouth."

Amber reached over to a table behind them and picked up the tape.

"No need. I'll stay quiet." Tripp's eyes widened. "Another word won't leave my mouth."

"Fine, but one more sound, and it's going back on," the guy growled as he turned and hurried to the window with his back facing us.

We need to head back before they catch our scent, Liam mind linked with me as he patted Evan's shoulder, nodding his head in the direction that we came from.

I'd expected Evan to resist, but he nodded, and the three of us retraced our steps.

After a few miles, Evan took a deep breath. "So that's your friend, right?"

"Yeah." I still couldn't believe that Tripp was the one they'd captured. "It doesn't make any sense. He would've told me he was in the rebellion."

"I'm not trying to be an asshole, but would he have, really?" Liam took my hand in his, and he squeezed it. "Look who your mate is?"

"I get that you would think that after how he acted right after we claimed one another, but he's one of my good friends." Tripp was happy-go-lucky and was loyal to a fault.

Or at least, I had thought he was. "There has to be an explanation."

"Regardless, we need to get him out of there sooner rather than later." Evan kept his pace as we hurried back to the dorms. "Once they feel they've gotten all the information out of him or that he's useless, they're going to make sure they get rid of the loose end."

"Wait, they're going to kill him?" I don't know why that thought hadn't even occurred to me yet.

"What did you expect them to do?" Evan glanced over his shoulder. "Let him loose to go back to classes. Tell everyone that the council had kidnapped him and tied him up. That wouldn't go over well."

"Don't be so hard on her." Liam took my hand and squeezed it. "We've known that part of our fathers for a long time; she's still new to our world."

"Well, she's your mate and needs to wake up." Evan kicked up his speed some more. "We need to get back and get some rest. Tomorrow is going to be a long day."

The thought of leaving Tripp there overnight didn't sit well. "Do you think we could attack in the morning?"

"No, we'll need to wait until nightfall again." Liam frowned at me. "And we have to go to class and act like nothing's wrong. Our dads are watching."

"But, what if he doesn't make it?" There must be something we could do right now.

"Our hands are tied until we have a plan," Evan said as we reached campus once more.

I'll text Bree and let her know what we found out. Liam glanced around to make sure there were no prying eyes. *That way, she'll see it as soon as she wakes up and will get the information to the Rebellion.*

It was a hard pill to swallow, but we did have to be

smart. *Okay.* The plan made sense even though I was feeling impatient ... reckless.

A short time later, we were back in the dorm, and we'd changed into our pajamas. As I crawled into bed next to Liam, my mind just played the scene over and over again. *Are you surprised that Amber is involved?*

No, I'm not. She's desperate to prove herself. Liam pulled me into his arms.

I laid my head against his chest. *You have a crazy-ass ex-girlfriend.*

His shoulders shook with laughter. *Fair enough. Now, close your eyes, and get some sleep.*

Even in his arms, there was a chill inside my bones. Tripp's face appeared each time I closed my eyes. He was one of my first friends here, and somehow he had gotten roped into this crazy world too. I needed to protect him, but here I was in a soft bed, in the arms of my mate. I was going to go free him tomorrow night with or without the rebellion's help.

CHAPTER FIVE

The alarm blared, startling me from my sleep. I'd been up tossing and turning all night and had only fallen asleep probably about an hour ago. I couldn't get the image of Tripp out of my mind.

I groaned as I reached over and turned off the alarm on my phone.

"Are you okay?" Liam tugged me back into his arms, making it even harder to get up.

"Yeah, I couldn't sleep." I didn't have to say anything else; he knew why.

"Well, let's get up and go talk to Bree." Liam released me and stood from the bed. "I'll call her now so she has time to become somewhat human before we get over there."

A small smile spread across my face. Bree was my best friend, and I loved her dearly. Hell, she even knew my secret that only Liam, Mr. Thorn, Max, and my parents knew. I trusted her that much, but she was not a morning person. "That's probably a very smart idea."

He winked at me, making my body heat.

"You keep looking at me like that, and we won't be going

to see my sister, and you might not make it to any of your classes," he said as he took a deep breath. He smelled my arousal.

I wanted to challenge him, but now wasn't the time. We had things that we needed to focus on. "I'll jump into the shower." Hopefully, that would make me wake up. I was going to need a strong cup of coffee today if not multiple cups.

As I entered the marble bathroom, I turned the water on in the rain shower, heating it as I went to grab some clothes for the day. I was glad that I didn't have any training with Evan today. I wasn't sure if I could make it through that given how little sleep I had.

It took about thirty minutes for me to get ready because I was still moving so slow. I had to put concealer under my eyes to hide the bags, which made my emerald eyes pop more. I left my long black hair down. When I stepped back into the bedroom as ready as I was going to be for the day, I found Liam sitting on the bed, waiting for me.

His eyes scanned over me, taking in my outfit as he stood and made his way over to me. "I'm one lucky man." A small grin played at the corners of his lips.

"Yes, you are." My heart fluttered at his words, and I brushed my lips to his. "Now you're wearing lip gloss."

He leaned down, pressed his lips to mine once more, and then pulled back. "Totally worth it."

I hoped he always made my heart skip a beat. With each day, I felt a little more for him than the last. "Let's go see your sister. We have a friend to save."

"All right." He licked his lips and took my hand. "Let's go." We walked out the door to find Evan pacing in the living room.

"It's about damn time," he grumbled and took a deep breath. "My patience was wearing thin."

I was getting worried about him. *That's not like him.* Ever since we left the abandoned factory yesterday, he'd been a little erratic.

Maybe it's stress. Liam nodded at the heir. "Calm down. We're ready to go. Calling them now won't make the night come any faster."

Evan didn't bother responding and opened the door to head into the hallway. "True, but the more time we all have to plan, the better."

Leave him alone. The last thing we needed was to aggravate Evan and have him go rogue like he had initially tried last night.

The rest of our way over to Sherry and Bree's dorm was made in silence. As soon as Evan knocked on their door, it opened.

Bree held the door open and waved us all in. Her hair was not the usual tangled mess, and her eyes seemed a little alive. "This better be good," she yawned.

The three of us marched in to find Sherry already dressed in her school uniform and ready for the day.

She sat on one of the recliners and smiled at us. "Good morning."

"Hey." I didn't want to be short, but I had to tell Bree about Tripp. "So, Evan figured out where they took the prisoner." I took a deep breath, unable to complete the sentence just yet. It was like, if I admitted it out loud, it'd become real, which was stupid.

"And..." Her eyes narrowed on me as she waited for an answer.

Liam wrapped an arm around my waist.

He gave me enough strength to say the next two words. "It's Tripp."

"Tripp?" Bree blinked a few times. "Our Tripp?"

"Yeah." I'd wondered why he hadn't been in class Monday, and I meant to give him a call. However, I had forgotten with everything else going on. I felt like such an ass. There was no telling how long he'd been there.

"How do you know this?" Her forehead lined with worry. "Maybe you got bad info."

"We saw him with our own eyes." Liam frowned as he took in both his sister's and my state.

I took a deep breath before sitting on the couch with Liam following right behind me.

"Where's your phone so we can text them the location?" Evan glanced around as if the phone would be sitting out in the open.

"It's in my room. I'll go grab it." Bree turned and hurried off to her bedroom.

"Someone dropped off my class schedule last night," Sherry said. "I wonder if we have any classes together. It's going to be hell catching up after everything I've missed." She held out a piece of paper in my direction.

I took a deep breath when I read through it. She had pre-calculus and shifter history with me. Those were the two classes I had with Tripp, and the classes had been full. Which could only mean that they removed him from the classes. Maybe it was someone other than Tripp. It had to be. "We have pre-calculus and shifter history together." I forced a smile. It wasn't her fault.

"Thank God." Her shoulders straightened. "It's nice knowing I'll at least have a few classes with someone I know."

That was something I understood so well.

Bree walked back into the living room and sat in the open recliner. "Okay, let's message them."

"Here, let me help." Evan hurried over to her and told her exactly what to type.

THE REBELLION HAD GOTTEN BACK to us immediately about what they had planned. They'd told us to stay behind and they'd tell us when the rescue was completed. Yeah, right. Like that was actually going to happen.

After that was settled, the five of us grabbed something to eat at the restaurant, and now Sherry and I were heading to class. Liam usually walked me, but he was meeting up with Micah and Simon to tell them about tonight's plan.

"So, what should I expect?" Sherry scanned the grounds as we approached the building. "Do we have to do anything crazy?"

"Did you go to a human school too?" I remembered being nervous about the same thing when I had started here.

"Yeah, I did." Her blonde hair bounced.

"Me too. But these classes are just like the ones you had there. There's not much of a difference at all, other than it's shifter history instead of the history we used to take."

"That's interesting though." She grinned. "My dad taught me things, but he was so busy, especially with Mr. Voss, those past few years."

I could only imagine.

We entered the classroom, and Robyn was already in her seat with her two minions. Her muddy brown eyes landed on me as she flipped her hair over her shoulder. She glanced at her friends and chuckled. "Something smells in here. It must be lingering from where you hung out while in New York. I heard you got the heirs to slum it with you too."

She was a stupid, heartless bitch. "Well, at least we took care of the residents instead of leaving them all to die and live in filth."

"They're weak. Who cares?" Robyn crossed her legs. "You're going to be the ruin of the heirs."

"And you and your daddy are ruining our people." I couldn't believe she had the nerve to throw down because she knew how they were living. Wouldn't pleading ignorance work better for her?

"Who cares as long as we stay on top?" Robyn smirked.

"If you care about being on top and not the value of the people underneath, you'll soon be left with no one." I didn't understand how they could be so cruel.

"People like her and her daddy get off on people suffering." Sherry turned her head and stared the bitch right in her eyes. "They're sick and sadistic like that."

"Ooh, looks like the loser found another friend," Robyn sneered.

Today wasn't the day to mess with me. "Apparently, she's found two." I pointed to her friend with the blue hair and purple eyes and then to her other friend, who chomped on her wad of gum with her pale green eyes shooting daggers at me.

"Not funny," Robyn growled.

"You're right, but I'm only as good as my audience." I hoped the bitch kept her mouth shut.

"Looks like I got here just in time." Professor Walker entered the room and, as usual, placed his briefcase down near the table. "In my class, we get along; otherwise, I have to send you to the council's office, and nobody wants that."

He paused for a second as his eyes landed on Robyn. "Well, sane people don't want that anyway."

Sherry chuckled as she pulled out her notebook.

Robyn's shoulder stiffened, but she didn't utter a word.

And then he began class as if everything was normal.

I TRIED to keep calm as the day progressed, but when I walked into Shifter History and found Tripp's seat vacant, I knew he wasn't coming back. "You can sit there."

"Hey, are you okay?" Sherry asked as she took his seat.

It was stupid. I wished he'd walk into the room and tell Sherry to vacate his seat. "No, I'm fine. It's just been a long day."

"I take it he was in these classes with you?" She laid her backpack at her feet and frowned. "I'm sorry."

"It's not your fault." She had nothing to apologize for. "At least, I still have a friend here with me."

A grin spread across her face. "I like the sound of that."

"So, apparently, Tripp has left Wolf Moon Academy, and we have a new student here to replace him." Professor Johnson walked into the room. "It's very unusual for a student to begin mid-semester, and it's probably best if I don't know the reasons why."

Now that I was watching him with the knowledge that he was my closest relative, I could see similar features to my father in him.

"I'd agree with that," Sherry said.

"Very well. Then, let's dive in." Professor Johnson pointed at me. "You will help her get caught up, right?"

"Of course." I'd do anything possible to ensure that

Sherry thrived here. The council would be looking for any excuse to release her from their program.

"Today, let's talk about protestors." He walked over and leaned against the whiteboard. "What do we know about protestors? If you look at Martin Luther King Jr., you'll see a peaceful man who made a change. But there are several other violent protestors out there as well. The same can be said about shifters."

"Well, the rebellion group would be considered protestors." Gertrude stated matter-of-factly. "They think they have something worth fighting for."

"You're right." Professor Johnson took a dry erase marker and opened it. "History has a way of repeating itself, but sometimes, it's wise to be patient." His eyes flickered to mine. "Being patient can let the monsters reveal themselves."

Those words were oddly specific for him to be throwing them my way. Or maybe, I was just being extra paranoid.

"Are you calling the council the monsters?" Asked the mouthy boy in the back row.

"No, but the rebellion group is." The professor shrugged. "Now, let's dive back into history."

WHEN CLASS WAS OVER, Sherry and I rose out of our seats and made our way toward the front door. *Hey, we're out of class.* I linked with Liam.

"I'm right here, waiting on you." Liam stepped into the doorway, and his eyes landed on me.

"Hey, you." I grinned as I stood on my tiptoes and pressed my lips to his. "I missed you this morning."

"See, I told you she was needy," Amber's words came from the hall.

My body stiffened at her words.

Ignore her. Liam kissed my lips once more. *It'll piss her off more. She's kind of like Simon that way.*

Okay, I can do that. I took a deep breath, steadying myself for it.

As we walked into the hallway, Amber's smug smile landed on me. "I love how you always prove me right."

Sherry moved to walk over to her, but I reached out and grabbed her arm.

She glowered at me for a second, but the three of us walked past Amber without pause.

"Hey, I'm talking to you," Amber yelled from behind.

Liam opened the door for us, and we walked out into the sun.

"Hey." She called again right before the door shut. "Hey!"

"Well, that was oddly satisfying." Sherry giggled as we hurried across the campus courtyard.

"She hates being ignored." Liam chuckled and took my hand in his. "Come on, we're all meeting up in Bree's dorm. Simon and Micah have been filled in, so we're all good to go."

"Okay, that sounds perfect." My shoulders dropped as I relaxed some. I didn't know if Simon would really be on board. "So, all six of us are going?"

"Uh. Seven." Sherry pointed at herself. "I'm part of the group now, and you can't leave me behind."

"But Simon doesn't want you to come." Liam shrugged his shoulders.

"I don't give a damn what he wants. I'll be there." Sherry

stomped. "It'll either be me leaving with you all, or I'm going on my own."

"Hey, you pick that fight with him and not me." Liam side stepped. "If I could, I'd get Mia to stay behind."

"But that won't work."

"Oh, I know." A sad smile filled his face. "And I respect it. I know he's important to you."

Damn right, we're breaking Tripp out tonight no matter what. I had a feeling we were going to see what the rebellion was truly made of.

CHAPTER SIX

W e were all hanging out at Sherry and Bree's dorm as we waited for midnight to ascend.

Simon was sitting in the recliner that faced the door as he continually glanced at Sherry, who was sitting on the side of the couch closest to him. Bree sat in the middle as Liam sat on her other side with me in his lap.

"We're going to have to play nice with the rebellion tonight." Evan tapped his foot as if he was anxious. "They don't even know we're showing up."

I wasn't sure what had gotten into him lately. He was normally cool, calm, and collected. Those three words defined him perfectly unless there was an actual visible threat in front of him, and right now, he was acting the opposite.

"I know that," Simon growled.

"I'm not sure you're helping your case." Micah carried a chair from the kitchen table into the room. "You're already sounding testy."

"Hey..." Simon started, but a loud knock on the door cut him off.

"Are we expecting someone?" Bree leaned forward.

"Uh, no." Sherry tapped her chin. "You guys are the only people I know or care to know."

"I've got it." Evan stood and headed to the door.

When he opened it, someone I hadn't seen in a while was standing there—Kai. His longish blond hair was styled in its usual unkempt way, and his sandy brown eyes met my own. He wore a black shirt and jeans that clung to his body perfectly. He had the playboy look down pat, a look that, at one time, I found alluring. He had tried to date me despite knowing that Liam was my mate, and I wound up hurting him. Fate did everything to not be ignored.

"Hey." He took in a deep breath as his eyes tore from me in Liam's arms to everyone else in the room. "I thought it'd be nice to stop by and check on you all."

"In clothes that aren't your uniform?" Evan questioned.

"Yeah, I had to run an errand and didn't want to wear academy clothes in the city." Kai glanced at the ground. "May I come in for a while?"

Liam's hands tightened around my waist. "Sure, for a little while."

"Really?" Simon rolled his eyes. "That prick was hitting on your girl."

"I'm very aware of that point," Liam's words were a growl. "But that's in the past; after all, he helped save her."

"Look, I'm not trying to cause problems," Kai said. "I wanted to see if you'd heard from Tripp. He hasn't been around in a while, and apparently, he unenrolled in the academy. That's not like him." His eyes weren't the warm color they usually were, and he was avoiding each one of our gazes.

He's hiding something. Liam linked with me.

I had to agree with him. "Well, you know as much as we

do." I was curious to see how he would play this. I never knew him to be manipulative, but right now, he was being pretty brazen.

"Tell us the truth. We know you're lying." Evan was a blunt kind of guy. I should've figured he would call him out.

"What?" His head snapped up, and he scanned the room. "No..."

"You smell rotten. You're omitting something, which is the same as lying. Did you forget we are all shifters?" Simon pinched the bridge of his nose. "Some people are morons."

The room became silent until Kai responded, "Okay, fine. I know what you're planning, and I want in."

"How is that possible?" Bree's eyebrows shot upward.

"Are you part of the rebellion?" Evan crossed his arms.

"Yeah, I am. It's not like I can lie." Kai blew out a breath and blinked.

"For how long?" It hurt that he hadn't been willing to tell me about this before.

"A while." He licked his bottom lip and sighed. "Look, they won't tell me where he's at, and I know you guys are helping." He paused as his brows furrowed. "Which, honestly, was something I never thought I'd say about them," Kai said as he pointed at the four heirs.

"Why won't they tell you?" Liam tilted to the side so he could see him clearly.

"Does it matter?" Kai huffed.

"Hell, yeah, it does." Simon shook his head and frowned. "If they don't want you, we don't want you."

"I agree with him." Micah nodded in Simon's direction.

"Now listen here," Kai said.

"No, they're right." Evan opened the door and waved his hand toward the hallway. "If you don't come clean, then we don't know what kind of liability you are on our hands, and it's a risk not worth taking."

"Mia." Kai glanced at me. "Help me, please."

Liam's hands tightened on my waist. *Of course, he's begging you.*

Stop. The last thing I wanted was for things to explode because of jealousy. "They're right. Come clean or you're not going."

"Bree?" Kai then looked at her.

She lifted both hands in the air. "This isn't up to me."

"Fine." His shoulders slumped, and he pointed at the door. "I'll tell you, so go ahead and shut it. No one needs to overhear this."

"Okay." Evan shut the door and made his way back to his spot on the recliner.

"First off, who's she?" Kai gestured at Sherry.

"Oh, I'm the new student from California." She held her hand out toward Kai. "My name is Sherry."

Kai reached over, and as soon as he touched her hand, Simon growled.

"I'm Kai." His forehead creased as he glanced at Simon. "It's odd for a student to join mid-semester."

"Stop being nosy, and get to the point." Simon's voice was raspy, and his body tense.

"Fine." Kai paced behind where Micah was sitting. "I may have been the one who got Tripp caught."

"What the hell?" Bree leaned forward in her seat like she was going to stand up.

"Give him a second." Sherry reached over and grabbed her arm. "It might sound worse than it really is."

"Either way, he's being held against his will, so it can't be much better." Bree wrinkled her nose in disgust.

"Look, I found out about the altar that you all found this

past weekend," Kai muttered. "They wanted me to do some investigating of my own, so Sunday night, I waited until close to midnight and snuck out into the woods."

"Let me guess; the idiot followed you." Bree's body sagged as if the fight in her was gone.

"Yes, he did, but I didn't know it." Kai rubbed a hand down his face. "I was too focused on making sure I didn't run into anybody, and honestly, he is kind of stealthy. I had no idea he was around until I heard a scream far away and smelled him on my return trip."

"A scream?" Sherry's brows furrowed.

"Yeah, I think he let himself get caught to save me." Kai frowned. "He's kind of stupid and loyal like that."

That sounded exactly like what might have happened. "So, why didn't you try to catch up with them?"

" I did." Kai pulled his bottom lip. "But Amber's scent was everywhere with his, and it disappeared like they had gotten into a car. So I need help getting him back. I think he did it for me."

"How does Amber keep getting involved?" The bitch just wouldn't go away.

"She's trying to make a spot for herself somewhere in the elites." Simon darkly chuckled. "She thought I was going to lock it down with her after you dumped her ass."

"I didn't dump her because we were never something to begin with." Liam's chest vibrated from an unheard growl.

"Okay, everyone needs to calm down." I stood and glanced at the clock. "It's time to go anyway."

Liam said, "She's right. Let's move." He stood beside me and took my hand.

Those words seemed to sober everyone up. Thank God.

"Wait, you aren't supposed to go. I just need you to tell

me where they're holding him." Kai frowned as he shook his head.

"One wrong move, Kai," Evan squared his shoulders as he got on both feet. "That's all it'll take for me to haul your ass away from there."

"Fine."

The eight of us used the stairwell, attempting to hide in the shadows. Even though we were all shifters, we were part human and enjoyed taking the elevator.

It only took a minute for us to get to the ground floor, and we snuck out the back door that led to the woods.

Evan took the lead, and soon, we were all sprinting to take cover in the trees. Once we all made it there, Evan held up a finger to his lips to indicate for us to be quiet.

My heart rocked inside my chest as my nerves came to a head. I didn't know what was wrong with me, but tonight, working with the rebellion and saving Tripp was taking its toll. Thankfully, the only sounds we heard came from the eight of us hiding.

"Let's go, but be quiet," Liam whispered as he took my hand and walked farther into the woods.

We were all moving relatively quickly. The moon was full and hanging high in the sky, and the woods were strangely quiet. Not even an owl made any noise. It was as if the animals knew what was about to happen.

As we drew closer, several scents blew in our direction. The rebellion members were already here, and there were at least five of them.

Be careful. Liam tugged my arm, making me slow down. *Remember the shit they pulled last night.*

I held my hand up, summoning the others to stop.

"So, you all decided to tag along." The girl's voice from the abandoned factory filled the air. "I'm actually surprised."

She emerged from among some thick branches, but this time, she wore a ski mask instead of a hoodie.

"It would've been nice if you would've informed us that it was a friend." I got that they didn't trust us, but they should've prepared us for something.

"Look, I didn't know he was your friend too." Her eyes landed on Kai. "Great, someone else who isn't supposed to be here."

"I came to save my friend." Kai bared his teeth at her. "Despite your protests, I need to be a part of the rescue team."

"If you were good at being a spy, we wouldn't be in this mess," she hissed as four large figures appeared and flanked her on both sides. All five of them wore similar ski masks.

The girl snarled. "Now, we have an untrained liability who could identify you as the person who went over the border."

"Willow, I messed up, and I want to make it right. I didn't mean for it to happen. I didn't know I was being followed." Kai clenched his hands into fists.

"You do realize you're not helping yourself, right?" It was weird to see him like this. When I had first met him, he seemed to have his act together, but not now.

"See, she even agrees with me, and now you've given them my name. You need to stick with a strategy." She tilted her head in my direction. "They can't know you're involved with us. That's why you need to turn around and go back."

"They aren't going down without a fight." Evan sneered. "So you should take all the help you can get."

"Your scent is going to be left behind." She crossed her arms as she faced off with us.

It was as if the elements were in our favor because a strong breeze began to blow.

"Not with weather like this." Liam pointed to the clouds rolling in. "A storm is coming."

"Fine, it's your ass if you get caught." The girl pointed to the road. "Okay, so we follow that gravel trail?"

"Yeah." Evan nodded, and he took a few steps toward her.

One of the men growled in warning. "Do not get close to her."

Evan stopped, and his mask of indifference slipped back into place. "What's the plan?"

"We should get closer before we make any plans." She took off, keeping to the trees. "Don't get left behind."

The now thirteen of us quietly walked through the woods. When we could make out the building, Willow paused and held up her hand. There were at least ten sentries tonight, all standing outside the small building on guard.

"Great, they must have caught your scent last night," Willow muttered as she turned around.

"If they had, the council would've done something." Bree's voice was only a whisper in the air.

"Not if it was faint and mixed with multiple scents." Willow's gaze landed on me. "I have a feeling Mia here was involved, and her mate wouldn't let her out of his sight." She turned her body so she was facing Evan. "And I bet he was the one who knew the location."

"Impressive, how'd you know?" Liam stepped slightly in front of me like they might be a threat.

"We'd heard of Mr. Rafferty keeping a place out in the woods somewhere near here, but we never were able to locate it... " A grin filled her face, "Until now."

"Well, it looks like it's good we came." Micah glanced back at the small building. "They have twice your numbers."

"We could still kick their asses," one of the huge men said.

"Like hell, you could," Simon growled.

"Now isn't the time to turn on each other." Sherry reached over and smacked Simon on top of the head. "You have got to learn that not everything is about you."

Bree giggled and clamped her hands over her mouth, trying to keep the sound in.

"Oh, dear God." Willow glanced over her shoulder at her men. "They are fucking children."

"Either way, you need us right now." I didn't like being talked down to, but we kind of deserved it at the moment. "So what's the plan?"

Willow's eyes moved back to the building. "We can't let them see any of you, so you'll each need to shift into your wolf and stay in the shadows. It's harder to tell who you are in animal form."

A loud crash of lightning sounded behind us.

"Mia and the other two girls can be the ones to help Tripp out." Willow motioned to Sherry. "I don't know you, so you aren't related to a council member, right?"

"No, I'm new here." Sherry waved her finger around to the heirs and me. "They saved me from an abusive alpha."

"That's another story that didn't make sense to me." Willow met Evan's eyes. "The fact that you all may actually care is surprising."

"Let's do this another time." We needed to get in there and get out fast. The storm would be a good cover and hide our scents.

"Fine, new girl stays in human form since they most likely won't recognize her." Willow took a deep breath. "That way, she can untie him. The four of you will need to run back where we met up earlier and stay hidden until we come back." She indicated Kai, Sherry, Bree, and me.

"What's going to happen if a guard recognizes us after tonight?" Bree popped her knuckles and sighed.

"Honey, those guards were trained to fight to the death." Willow arched an eyebrow. "None of them is going to survive tonight."

Her words made sense, but I hadn't even considered that possibility. Tonight, we weren't just saving a friend; we were declaring war.

CHAPTER SEVEN

The breeze picked up even more as we slowly moved but remained hidden in the woods as we got closer to the building. It was as if the elements could sense what was coming... what was starting.

One of the guards moved slightly so Tripp came into view. He was still stuck in that seat but was leaning over to the side. I hoped it was from sleep and not from something else.

Willow and Evan were in the lead with Liam and me following directly after them as the others lagged a little behind. We continued to remain quiet so the guards would stay unaware for as long as possible.

"We're going to move inside when the rain starts, right?" The guards from the corner glanced at the one closest to the woods where we were hiding.

"We need at least a couple to stand guard outside to listen for anything." The man closest to us chuckled. "And it damn sure won't be me."

They were distracted, which was a good thing.

Willow glanced over her shoulder at the group and pointed to the tree line. It was time to fight.

Someone patted Liam's shoulder, and we both turned to find Micah holding his hand out. He pulled out a necklace that was hidden under his shirt and unclasped it.

Understanding filled Liam's eyes. *He wants our dorm key so we don't lose it after we shift.*

That's smart. For whatever reason, I hadn't even considered that we would shift into our wolves. However, it only made sense that we would.

While Liam handed him the key, Willow and the others were already shifting. Hair sprouted all over their skin, and soon their clothes ripped as they went down onto four legs.

Let's go. Liam said as he called his wolf forward.

Within seconds, our group of wolves headed to the tree line.

"Do you hear something?" The guard closest to us glanced at the tree line, and his eyes widened when he obviously caught our scent. "We've got activity," he yelled.

That's what we wanted. We needed them to be drawn away from the building so Sherry, Bree, and I could easily get to Tripp while the others distracted them.

I turned, passing by the others until I reached Bree and Sherry. Bree's wolf was identical to Liam's but smaller. It made me realize that I'd never run with her before.

"Get ready." Sherry's voice was so light that the wind carried it away, but I still heard it.

A gun shot off toward our group as an auburn wolf jumped out and attacked the closest guard.

"What the hell?" One of the other guards ran over to him, and he must have seen the rest of them in the woods. As he stumbled back, a loud howl filled the air.

"We're under attack," one of the guards yelled as he aimed his gun toward Evan.

No. I ran in their direction when Sherry stepped into my path. "We have to get Tripp. Then we can help."

She was right. We needed to focus on saving Tripp first.

The guards ran to the woods as the rest of the wolves attacked. Gunshots sounded as the fighting began.

It was the hardest thing to watch my friends fight while I stood on the sidelines. When each guard was fighting a wolf, Sherry waved us on, and we ran out of the tree line for the building.

No one noticed as we ran past them, and soon we'd reached Tripp. Thankfully, the glass door was left open again.

"Hey," Sherry whispered as we approached him. "We're here to save you."

"Huh?" Tripp's head bobbed from one side to the other.

"We're here to save you." Sherry touched his shoulder for a second as she tried to get him to wake up.

It'd be a whole lot easier if he was conscious.

She glanced around before running over to the desk we hadn't noticed against the wall. She slowly opened the drawer, but it still made a loud groaning noise.

Shit. They had to have heard that.

Footsteps pounded on the ground as two more guards appeared from the opposite side of the woods. As they ran by the sliding glass door, they stopped in their tracks when they saw me.

"They're trying to break him out," the taller guard said.

"No shit." The other one pulled his gun from his pocket.

Great, another chance for me to get shot. My heart was racing, but I couldn't let panic take over my thoughts. I couldn't let anyone get hurt. I pushed off of my legs, allowing my wolf to take over. He lifted the gun to aim it at me, and I ran to the side as he pressed the trigger, narrowly missing me. Before he could take another shot, I jumped and aimed for his throat.

He lifted his hands to his shoulders and pushed me off of him, making both me and the gun fall to the floor.

A loud growl sounded before Bree launched toward the second guard as he went for his gun. Her mouth clamped down on the hand that was pulling the gun from his holster.

"Ow, dammit!" he yelled.

As the guard I was fighting scrambled on the floor for his gun, I threw caution to the wind and went for his throat once more. He hadn't expected me to recover so quickly, and I caught him off guard. My teeth sank into his throat, and I jerked my head, ripping his throat out. He wobbled for a second before falling to the floor.

His warm blood coated my mouth as I blinked several times with the realization of what I'd done.

"Mia, Bree needs help," Sherry said, waking me from whatever spell I'd fallen under. I couldn't fall apart right now. I'd done it out of self-preservation, not for sport. Though I knew that it should've made me feel better, it didn't.

Taking a deep breath, I turned to find the other guard holding Bree up by the neck.

"You stupid bitch," his words were filled with such hate. "You're going to pay for what you've done."

I rushed over and stood on my hind legs so I was tall enough to bite into his arm. I saw where Bree had already bitten him only moments ago and bit into the exact same spot, clamping down hard.

"Ow." He kicked his leg into my stomach, knocking the breath out of me.

Despite my head becoming light, I didn't release my hold.

His hands slackened against Bree's neck, and she crumpled to the ground.

The guard used his uninjured arm to grab me by the neck, choking me like he'd just done to Bree. I couldn't let him get the best of me though.

I rocked my wolf body forward, digging my claws into his chest and stomach.

He jerked me to the side, trying to get my claws to retract from his body, but I dug in deeper, making sure they stayed. Blood seeped from the cuts, and his eyes began to glaze.

All of a sudden, Bree stood up, regaining her balance on all fours, and jumped at his throat, hitting the mark perfectly. He stumbled back as his grip on my neck slackened. Soon, he dropped me as he tried pushing Bree off him but with no luck.

She didn't rip his throat out like I had done to the other guy but, instead, let him bleed out with her teeth remaining locked in place.

"Tripp, wake up." Sherry sounded desperate.

I turned around, watching as Sherry finished untying the last rope, setting him free. However, Tripp just sat there in a daze. Sherry drew her hand back and slapped him hard across the face.

"Ow." His eyelids fluttered open, and his hand jerked to his cheek. "What the hell!" Then, he looked around. "Holy shit. You're rescuing me." He rushed to his feet, and then his forehead creased. "Who are you?"

"It doesn't matter." Sherry grabbed his arm so she could pull him to the door. "Right now, we need to get you to safety."

Bree whimpered as she let go of the guard's neck and stood in front of us. She nodded in the direction we'd come from.

"Let's go." Sherry kept her grip on Tripp's arm as she tugged him to the sliding glass door. "Be quiet. We're going to hide in the woods."

"Uh, okay." He stumbled a little as if he was disoriented or possibly something worse.

The three of them ran toward the woods while I stayed behind. They were going to get pissed when they realized I hadn't gone with them.

I rushed to the side where the rest of the group was fighting the guards, only to find two of the men from the rebellion dead on the ground.

Holy shit. This was bad.

I searched for Liam. He was on all fours and fighting a guard with someone from the rebellion. The wolf was slightly smaller than the other ones surrounding them, so it was Willow. Her red fur was the same color as blood.

I glanced behind me as I watched Tripp and the girls make it back into the woods. At least, they were safe for the time being.

A low growl filled the air right behind me. I turned around to find a wolf I didn't know, who locked his eyes with mine. Saliva dripped from his mouth as he slowly stalked toward me.

Mia, what the hell are you doing? Liam stopped for a second and looked my way. *You were supposed to go with the others.*

I wasn't about to leave you. If he thought I was going to run away and hide while they risked their lives, he had lost his damn mind.

The wolf slowly stalked toward me as if he was enjoying

the hunt. He wanted me to feel like I was his prey and tried his best to mess with my mind.

I lifted my head in indifference and tried giving him a wolfy smile.

It must have worked because his eyes narrowed directly on me, and he charged.

At the last second, I lowered onto my belly, making him stumble over me. When his body hit my back, I stood on my hind legs, which caused him to crash into the ground due to his momentum.

A deep, raspy sound vibrated from his chest as he stood back up and stared at me.

He clawed at the dirt as he took in a deep breath. Right when he was about to charge, Liam jumped for him, ripping out his throat.

When the wolf went down, an eerie silence filled the air as rain started dropping from the sky.

Willow and the others had shifted back into human form and changed into the extra sets of clothes they had brought.

The heirs, Bree, Kai, and I were still in wolf form when they had made it back to us.

"We have to bury the dead and then he," Willow said as she pointed to Tripp, "must come with us."

Kai growled.

"If he goes back, the council will just capture him again. He'll only be safe with us." Willow hadn't even bothered trying to hide her appearance now. Her dark red hair fell to her shoulders, and her blue eyes found mine. "The rest of you need to head back so no one notices that you were gone."

She was right. The longer we stayed out here, the more difficult it would be.

"I'll be calling you tomorrow." Willow met Bree's eyes. "Have your phone near you."

Come on, let's get back. Liam motioned to the others as we turned to head back to Wolf Moon.

As I turned, Tripp stopped next to me. "Thank you." His eyes twinkled with unshed tears as he patted my head and then followed after Willow.

Since I didn't want to have a meltdown, I nodded at him and headed home.

AFTER WE'D GOTTEN BACK and settled, I stood in the shower, letting the hot water run over me. Every time I closed my eyes, I could see the wolf I had killed over and over again. Even the metallic taste of his blood still filled my mouth.

"Hey, are you okay?" Liam entered the bathroom with concern.

"I don't know." I didn't want to tell him what I had done. What if he thought differently of me? I turned the water off and grabbed a towel, trying to keep myself occupied so I wouldn't close my eyes and cry. As I put my clothes on, Liam turned toward me.

"Bree called me and told me what happened." Liam leaned back on the door and watched me.

Of course, she told him. I finished putting my clothes on and turned toward him. "I don't want to talk about it." My voice cracked at the last word.

"You know you didn't do anything wrong, right?" Liam

took a step toward me and took hold of my hand. "If you hadn't killed him, he would have killed you."

"He was still someone's son and, hell, maybe even a husband or father." What if he had a little kid at home, waiting for their daddy to come home?

"You can't do that." Liam pulled me into his arms and held me tightly despite my soaking wet hair. "You weren't doing it for pleasure. You did what you had to do to survive." Regret poured through our bond. "I should've gone with you."

"No, you shouldn't have." The guards had guns, and the rebellion needed everyone available to help them. Luckily, we were being extra cautious by separating so Bree and I went with Sherry. It would've turned out badly if we hadn't.

"Does it ever get easier?" He'd killed tonight too. It wasn't like I was the only one.

"No, it doesn't." He ran his fingers through my hair. "You'll never forget it, and you have to work through your emotions. But you also have to think about what would've happened if you hadn't done what you did."

He was right. If I hadn't killed him, then Bree would have fought the other guy alone and might not have made it out alive which meant Sherry and Tripp wouldn't have either. It changed my perspective some, but it still didn't feel right. "I see your point, but..."

"I'm not saying you have to be okay with what you did." Liam kissed my forehead. "I'm saying don't beat yourself up so much." He released me and took my hand, tugging me into the bedroom. "The best thing we can do right now is lie down and maybe watch something funny on television."

He crawled into bed and lay down, holding his arms out to me. "Let's cuddle, watch a show, and just take it day by day."

Day by day. That sounded a whole lot easier than the rest of my life.

I climbed into bed and laid my head on his shoulder. With his free arm, he turned the TV on and flipped through the channels until he found something good.

I took a deep breath, absorbing his comforting scent of musk and sandalwood. I could do this. I only had to get through the night. Surely that wouldn't be difficult.

CHAPTER EIGHT

After getting dressed and ready for the day, I stood in the bathroom, staring at my reflection in the mirror. I'd had nightmares all night where I relived killing that guard over and over. I was able to hide the dark circles under my eyes, but my emerald eyes didn't sparkle like they used to. Hell, maybe it was just my imagination. I wore a blood-red sports bra underneath a silver Wolf Moon Academy tank top with matching blood-red exercise shorts and had braided my hair.

"Hey, let's go to the restaurant and grab some breakfast." Liam brushed his fingers against my bare arm.

It's funny because it'd been a while since we'd eaten there. Now that I'd thought about it, I hadn't yet with Liam as a couple. "Yeah, okay." I wasn't hungry, but maybe getting me out and around people would make me feel a little better.

"Great, Sherry and Simon are going to meet us there." Liam's lips curved upward at the corners like he was trying to hide a smile.

Those words were enough to snap me out of my funk at least temporarily. "What?"

"Yeah, Simon called me this morning and asked for us to meet them." Liam finished buttoning the top button on his silver shirt. "They may already be there. I didn't want to rush you."

"I'll be okay." I couldn't lie and tell him I was fine now. First off, it wouldn't work, he'd both feel and smell my lie; and secondly, I wanted to ensure our relationship was always open and honest. "Let's go."

He pulled me into his arms and pecked my forehead. *I love you.*

Warmth spread across my chest, relieving me of the cold feelings left over from my dreams. *I love you too.*

Let's go before I throw you on the bed and take you like I want to. He released me from his arms and took my hand.

Maybe I want you to. My body heated in response to his words.

A deep growl left his chest. *If you weren't going to training, I would be taking you up on that offer, but you need to eat.*

I wanted to pout, but he was right. I planned on making Evan kick my ass today. "Fine."

He chuckled as we headed out the door.

Within minutes, we were walking into a packed restaurant. It was the only place to eat on campus unless you cooked in your dorm. I glanced at the booths that lined the walls, and Sherry leaned out of the one in the back right corner to wave us over.

"There they are." I tugged on Liam's arm as we weaved through the tables that were strategically scattered inside.

"Oh, my God." Robyn's nasally voice hit my ears like a freaking sledgehammer. "She won't give up."

"Don't worry about her," Amber responded as we were passing by their table of four. "He'll be crawling back to me any minute now."

I was so sick and tired of being talked down to. I stopped in my tracks and turned toward them. "God, you are pathetic." I took a deep breath and glanced from Robyn back to Amber. "They want nothing to do with either of you. Yeah, maybe you got to spread your legs for Liam and Simon, but not anymore. The more you two act like this, the worse you look because everyone knows that you two will amount to nothing."

"What?" Amber jerked back as if she had been slapped.

Dear God, didn't they realize they were blessed to not have to be raised like normal people or as an elite. They acted like they were being mistreated or worse, but they had everything handed over to them on a silver fucking platter. "Move on. None of us want to be around any of you."

"Liam, she makes you look weak." Amber's eyes landed on my mate.

"To whiny, entitled bitches like you?" He stared down his crazy ex-girlfriend. "She's my fated, and we've claimed each other. I don't know how much clearer it could be for you."

"But..."

"There aren't any buts." If she thought I was going to continue to let her act this way, she'd lost her damn mind.

An evil laugh came from the booth we were heading to that was only two tables away. Simon leaned forward, and I saw a coldness to him that I had forgotten he possessed. "You were nothing to us but a toy to play with. Now, you're just useless. Quit wasting our precious time."

"Aw, that sucks for you." Robyn smirked at Amber.

"Maybe you don't deserve to be sitting with us since you've clearly been written off."

"And you honestly think you're much better?" Simon tilted his head as he took the girl in. "We only used you one time to get back at her," he said as he pointed at me, "Now, we want nothing to do with you."

"He's right." Liam wrapped an arm around my waist and wrinkled his nose. "None of you matter. It's about damn time you figured it out. Let's stop wasting our precious time on them and join our friends." He pointed over to Sherry and Simon.

"Gladly." I turned and kissed his lips before pulling back and heading to the table.

The whole section of the restaurant had become silent as they watched the show. I had no clue until that moment.

"Wow, and I thought I knew how to make an entrance." Sherry chuckled as I slid into the booth first, sitting across from Simon.

"I think it's something we're all blessed with now." Us being part of the heirs' group gave me a lot more attention than I'd ever had before. I wouldn't give Liam up for the world, but sometimes I wished life could be a little simpler.

"So what do we owe the pleasure of you taking our side?" Liam arched an eyebrow at Simon.

"Hey, I might've been combative before, but I know who I need to stick close to," Simon replied as he took Sherry's hand. "Besides, you guys were right for listening to her."

I blinked several times to make sure my eyes weren't playing tricks on me. After a second, I took a deep breath, and my mouth dropped open. "Holy shit, you guys are bonded."

Liam slid in beside me and placed his arm around my shoulders. "It's about time."

"Hey, I had to let it process." Simon lifted both hands in the air. "At least, I didn't take as long as you did."

He's got you there. It was amazing, Simon seemed like a different person. He appeared grounded if that was even possible for him.

"What made you have a change of heart?" I was happy for them both, but I'd figured it would take even longer for Simon to be okay with it.

"Last night." Simon wrapped his arm around Sherry as he sighed. "I saw that wolf charge her, and thankfully, you saved her since I was too far away. I figured it was pointless to keep fighting it. After all, Liam seems so much happier now than he ever had been, so it couldn't be as bad as our dads told us."

"Your parents are assholes." Sherry cuddled against Simon's arm. "And they want you to be assholes like them. That's why they didn't want you to mate with your fated."

"That's true." I hadn't considered it like that, but she probably hit the nail on the head. "Fated mates are meant to ground us."

"It doesn't matter now." Liam leaned over and kissed my cheek. "We're all here and together."

And for the first time, everything seemed normal.

BEFORE I KNEW IT, Saturday was here. I was over at the dorm, hanging out with Bree and Sherry since the guys were already getting ready for their game tonight. Luckily, it was off-campus at a school only thirty minutes away, so we'd get at least a little break from Wolf Moon.

"I'm kind of excited." Sherry grinned. "This will be the first college game I've ever been to."

"Well, I'm kind of excited myself. Nate and Max are going to come. This is KSU's off week." Bree clapped her hands as she walked into the living room to grab her purse and keys from the table. "Are you two ready to go?"

I was more than ready. She'd forced me to change into a long-sleeve Wolf Moon Academy shirt and jeans. I'd hoped to go wearing neutral clothes, but apparently, that wasn't possible. Then she did my makeup, coloring my eyelids silver and my lips blood-red. Luckily, I was able to pull it off with my skin tone and black as night hair.

Sherry had been forced into the same thing. However, for some reason, Bree let her get away with a more natural look, and I was so damn jealous.

"Are you sure you don't want to drive?" I was afraid to drive Liam's car. It was a brand new Escalade, and with my luck, I'd hit a boat again or something.

"First off, Liam would never allow me to drive his car; and secondly, my car is a two-seater." Bree pressed the button on the key fob that hung on the key chain I was holding. "So, this is on you."

"Fine." I took a deep breath and then blew it out.

Within minutes, we were piled into the car, and I was pulling out of the school.

"This is like driving a freaking truck," I growled as I took a turn, feeling as if the car might tilt over.

"Hey, calm down," Sherry said from the seat behind me. "You're doing okay."

"The more you drive it, the more you'll get used to it." Bree winked at me.

The next thirty minutes felt like hours as I finally found a parking spot I could actually pull into. It was about a mile away from the stadium, but we could use the walk. The game started in an hour.

"Finally." Bree jumped out of the passenger side front. "Maybe I should drive us back."

"I'd be all for it." I shut the driver's side door as Sherry climbed out through the door right behind me.

"Okay, I'm letting Nate know where we are." She pulled her phone from her pocket and began texting.

The three of us joined the mass of people heading to the game.

Her phone immediately buzzed back, which wasn't surprising. She glanced at the message and stopped in her tracks, causing the man behind her to bump into her.

"Hey, watch it." The guy grumbled as he slid past her and headed toward the stadium.

"Is everything okay?" Her reaction had me worried.

"They want to meet us at a bar outside the stadium." She glanced around as if she was looking for Nate to pop out and say hey.

"Why? We need to get to the game and get seated." Sherry frowned. "I told Simon I'd be there for warm-ups."

"I don't know, but let's go drag them out." Bree shrugged as she plugged in the place on her phone and headed that way. "They were probably pre-gaming while they waited on us."

"Okay, let's hurry." That did sound like something they would do.

The three of us headed off in the direction of the bar. Luckily, it wasn't too far away, and it was buzzing with college-aged students.

When we entered the place, my eyes landed on Max right away. He was talking to some girl with dark red hair. When she turned around and locked eyes with me, I knew exactly who it was.

Willow.

"Why is she here?" I asked as I glanced over at Bree, whose mouth hung open.

"I... I don't know." She lifted a hand. "I swear."

"Are they part of it?" Sherry pursed her lips.

"No, Max would tell me." I paused. "Right?"

"That's something between the two of you." Bree took a deep breath as the three of them headed our way.

Great, that was my answer right there.

Hey, are you okay? Liam's voice filled my head. *You seem upset. Are you almost here?*

I'm fine. I hated to worry him, but he'd get pissed if I didn't tell him. *We stopped at a bar to grab Nate and Max, but it'll take a minute. Willow is here.*

What? His voice held concern. *Where are you? I'll be right there.*

No, you've got a game. The council was already pissed. The heirs had been summoned about an incident. They didn't tell the heirs the specifics, but we knew what they were referring to. Their fathers suspected a spy in their midst, so we didn't need to draw any more attention to ourselves. *Your parents will get suspicious of you.*

"Let's go outside," Willow whispered as she walked past, heading out the door, followed by Nate and Max.

Here we go, I needed Liam to focus on the game while I figured out what was going on. *Fine, but if something bad goes down, let me know immediately.* It was clear by his words and through our bond that he wasn't thrilled with me going without him.

I'll let you know when we get there. I looped my arm through Sherry's and pulled her in the direction of the others.

We stepped outside and found the three of them across

the street, away from people. I took a deep breath and headed over to them.

"Hey." Max smiled at me as he ran his hands through his dirty blond hair, and Willow noticed me.

Max wrapped me in his arms. "It's good to see you, sis."

"Good to see you." I tried to calm down. "This is Sherry. She's new to Wolf Moon."

"Oh, is she the girl you saved from that one pack?" Nate's brown eyes were warm. He placed his arm around Bree and kissed her lips.

"Yeah, the very one." Sherry grinned but seemed a bit unsure.

I pulled back from Max and pointed at him. "This is my brother and he," I said as I pointed at Nate, "is Nate if you hadn't figured that out."

"Yeah, hey." Sherry focused on Willow. "I didn't expect to see you here."

"That's the whole reason." Willow grinned, and her attention landed on me. "I was hoping I could talk to you."

"Well, I'm here." She wanted to talk to me away from the other heirs. "Let's go for it."

"Fine. Another one of our comrades got caught." Willow lifted her head.

So it was official; Max was involved with them. "Why didn't you tell me?" Right now, that was more important than whatever she said.

"The same reason why you didn't tell me." Max crossed his arms, ready for a fight. "I wanted to protect you."

"Fine." He had a point even if I didn't like it. "So, you need us to find out where they are?"

"No." She shook her head. "We need you to get the layout of the building. We can't chance any of you getting caught."

"What building is it?" Bree's forehead creased.

"It's one in Chicago." Willow let the words settle before she spoke again. "We need to get him out before they execute him. It's the shifter headquarters there."

"I'll get it from Liam." I had no clue how to get it, so he would need to help me.

"Are you sure about that?" Nate frowned at me.

"They already know me from the rescue mission with Tripp." Willow glanced at him from the corner of her eye. "Besides, I know who she is. If she trusts them, then so do I."

Her words hit me in the gut. She knew I was the Overseer. If she did, then who else could know?

CHAPTER NINE

When Sherry and I arrived back at the dorm, I paced in circles. Wolf Moon had dominated the game, so everyone was in high spirits except for me. Willow's words haunted me. She knew who I was. How? Did Bree tell Nate? For some reason, my gut told me no. Then who?

Our bus is almost back home. Liam's words popped into my mind. *The guys want to go to a party tonight.*

I'm not up for it. I hadn't told him yet. *All six of us need to talk.*

We'll be there in a few minutes. He didn't ask any questions, which I was thankful for. I was afraid he might try to talk me out of it, but we had to tell the other heirs before they found out from someone else. That kind of information needed to come directly from the source... me.

"Hey, are you okay?" Sherry sat on one of the recliners as she stared at me. "You've been quiet ever since we met Willow outside the bar. Are you worried you can't get the information?"

That should be bothering me, but it wasn't. I had a

feeling Liam would know what to do with that one. "Let's wait on the others."

"Well, Bree might not be back until the morning." Sherry cringed like she was telling me something I'd forgotten.

"No, we don't need her for this." That sounded way worse than I had meant for it to, but Sherry seemed to understand what I meant.

There was a knock on the dorm door so I turned and opened it. When Liam appeared before me, it was like the air had been knocked out of me. He still gave me butterflies. "Hey."

His eyes twinkled. "Hey, you." *Now, what's wrong?*

"Gross." Micah groaned as he walked past me. "They're like eye fucking right in front of us."

Evan chuckled as he and Simon entered the room behind Micah.

It's time for my secret to come out. I stood and kissed his lips. The smell of sweat and his musk had my mind thinking things that were definitely not appropriate at the moment. I had to focus on the task at hand. *Willow knows, and they need to hear it from us.*

How the hell does she know? He took my hand and shut the door behind him.

No clue. We need to figure it out, but until then, we need to tell them. I knew that this would have to happen eventually, but I hadn't expected it to be so soon. I still didn't have my head wrapped around it, but sometimes, time wasn't on our side.

Simon grabbed Sherry's waist and picked her up as he took her spot in the chair. He then placed her on his lap.

"Hey, who said I was okay with that?" She giggled as she said the words.

Micah took the other recliner as Evan sat on one end of the couch.

Evan's intuitive eyes landed on me. "What's going on?"

"Well, we ran into Willow tonight prior to the game." I wasn't quite sure what Liam had told them if anything. He didn't know what had happened either.

"Really? She has some nerve since she never called the next day like she said she would." Simon shook his head.

"What did she want?" Liam asked as he took my hand and pulled me to the couch.

I sat down in the middle, between Evan and Liam. "Apparently, someone important to the rebellion was caught, and he's being kept at shifter headquarters in Chicago. They need to know how the place is set up to do a rescue mission."

"We could just do it." Micah crossed his arms as he sat back. "It'd probably be better that way."

"And easier for one of us to get caught, too." Evan frowned and leaned back. "They need us to stay close to our dads."

"But do we want to give them inside information on one of the headquarters?" Micah bit his bottom lip. "I mean, they could use it for God knows what."

"I think this is another test." It had to be. They were testing our loyalties.

"How so?" Sherry's forehead wrinkled.

"Because if we're part of their group, then we would be willing to hand over any information that we have." Evan leaned back and took a deep breath.

"So, they're seeing if we're all in or not." Liam's body tensed ever so slightly before it relaxed once more.

"We're all in, right?" Sherry grimaced like she was afraid of what the answer would be.

"I am." I could only speak for myself. "We've seen what the packs are going through. To turn a blind eye would be worse than not doing anything."

"She's right, and I'm in, too." Liam took my hand in his and squeezed it gently. "And I can give them the information right now. Or I can draw it out."

"Hell, at this point, I'd thought we were all in." Micah glanced around the room. "I mean we even killed some of our own guards."

"Yeah, you're right. And after seeing what happened to Sherry, I don't want to see anyone else suffer like that." Simon's words were filled with guilt. "It took me a little while to finally understand that."

"Then, we're agreed." Evan nodded.

My phone dinged from my pocket. I pulled it out and found the following text -

Send us the information as soon as you find it. - W

Max must have given her my phone number. I was a little relieved since we didn't have to rely only on Bree for communication now.

"Who is it?" Liam read the note.

"Willow." I took a deep breath.

"Let me get something to draw with then," Liam said as he got up, but I tugged him back down.

"That's not all." My heart pounded in my chest.

"Okay, what else?" Micah's forehead creased. "We can't do too much at one time or we'll get caught."

"No, it has nothing to do with another mission." Things were crazy. "It's something about me."

You don't have to do it. Liam squeezed my hand. *We can wait until you're ready.*

I don't know if I'll ever be. I had to tell them. They

deserved to know. It didn't only affect Liam and me. "But first, I need you all to promise to keep this secret until it's the right time for it to come out."

"Are you sick?" Sherry asked with concern.

"No, no it's not that." I wasn't trying to scare them. "I just need you all to promise me that this stays a secret between us and only us."

"Fine, we promise." Simon shrugged his shoulders.

I glanced at each one of them, and they nodded in agreement.

"Okay." I forced the next words out. "Brent Forrest." I started with the name because it was still so damn painful to get it all out in one sentence. My father, who I'd never met, had died trying to make things right for me.

"The dead Overseer?" Evan's brows furrowed as he glanced at Liam and then me.

"Yeah, the very one," Liam said as he pulled me closer to him. *I'm right here.*

I stared at my and Liam's joined hands. "He was my father." I took a deep breath and lifted my gaze to them.

"That's fucking impossible." Simon blinked a few times like he couldn't believe what he had heard. "He died without an heir. I was right about you all along; you're fucking with us."

"No, I'm not." I tried to stay calm despite his attitude and replayed the story that my mom had told me. "They'd just found out that they were expecting the night of his death."

"But you're a pack alpha's daughter." Micah scratched the back of his neck. "Have you been lying to us this whole time?"

"No, I didn't know until recently. The pack alpha is my stepfather." Saying it out loud sounded so weird. He was my father in all ways except biological. "I grew up with him being my real father."

"This is crazy and really convenient." Simon's voice turned cold. "Something a manipulative bitch would do."

"Let her talk." Sherry held compassion as she tried reeling her mate in.

"Why are you telling us now, and how long have you known?" Evan didn't seem surprised but almost resolved. "Something had to prompt it. You aren't telling us out of the goodness of your heart."

"I'd always planned to tell you, I just had to know we were in it together." They knew I was speaking the truth. They could smell otherwise. "I learned the day after Liam and I claimed one another. Once we all agreed that we were all in, I knew I needed to tell you soon. But after Willow made a reference tonight, cluing me in that she knew who I was, I realized it needed to be sooner rather than later."

"How the hell does she know?" Micah frowned and leaned forward in his chair. "Who all have you told before us?"

"That's bullshit." Simon's words were loud and his jaw clenched. "You told them before us."

"Oh, shut it." Sherry glanced over her shoulder at him and then stood. "You were an asshole. Hell, you still are, just not quite as bad. How would you've handled the news just a week ago?"

Simon closed his eyes and huffed. "Not well."

"See." Sherry tapped her foot on the ground. "She was right to wait."

"The only other person outside of Liam, my parents, and brother who know is Bree." I paused, hating that I dropped this on them.

"You talk a good game, but I bet you can't prove it."

Simon lifted his chin. "Throwing around that word doesn't make it true.

"She doesn't..." Liam started, but I held a hand up.

"Yes, she does." Evan's tone was low and dark. "Do you know how big of a deal this is? If we can't prove it, it'll ruin us."

"No, if they want proof. I have something." I headed toward my bedroom and grabbed my pendant and a picture of my father that my mom had given me the last time I visited. I took a moment to collect my thoughts and walked back into the room." I let the necklace dangle from my fingertips.

"No fucking way." Evan stood and took it from me. "That was the original crest."

"And this." I held out a picture of my father and mom, smiling at the camera as they held up a positive pregnancy test. My eyes burned with unshed tears.

"Holy shit, it's true." Micah looked like he'd been run over by a truck. "You're saying that we have a full fucking council sitting here, and you're only just now telling us?"

"Yes, but we're not sharing this." Liam glared at the southern heir. "You promised."

"They aren't going to hand it over to us any sooner than they have to." Evan paced.

That was one thing I could always count on. Evan continually seemed to be on the same page as Liam and me. "It's something we need to use as an ace up our sleeve later. Not now."

"Right. We're going to have to set it up in a way that makes it so they have to hand it over." He paused and met my eyes, his darkening. "Is there anything else you need to tell us?"

His words hurt, but I deserved it. He'd been loyal to me

first, and I hadn't trusted him with my burden. "I think Kai's dad might have an inkling."

"What?" Simon's words were high pitched. "Why do you say that?"

"I wore the pendant one day. I didn't realize its meaning, and Kai's dad was visiting on campus and saw it." A memory of my last words with him in Chicago when we were doing the weeklong tour haunted me. "He alluded to knowing who I was."

"But the rebellion wouldn't know that. He wouldn't have given up that information." Micah bit his thumb. "Hell, he couldn't stay with us because he was dealing with them."

"I know, so I'm not sure who told the rebellion." I hated to admit it, but everything led back to Bree.

"Right now, that doesn't matter." Liam huffed.

"Hell, yeah, it does." Evan looked over at him. "They have blackmail over us."

For some reason, I didn't think they would use it.

"Even if it's true, we are on their side. So they can't blackmail us to do the very thing we were going to do anyway. And right now, the first step is getting whoever it is out of the headquarters." Liam stood and headed over to the kitchen, looking for pen and paper. "Let's do this."

THE NEXT FEW days passed without anything out of the ordinary happening. Sherry and I were making our way to our training session when we ran into Mr. Rafferty and Evan heading in the direction of the school.

"Are we not training today?" My words faded off at the end when I took in Mr. Rafferty's expression.

His face was set in a scowl, and his body was so strained that the veins in his neck popped out. "No, you're not. But you two are required for this meeting as well."

"For what?" Sherry's brows furrowed.

"You'll find out soon enough. The other council members are rounding up the others now." He pointed toward the building that housed the council meeting room.

Mia, I think they must have gotten whoever it was out of the headquarters. Liam's strong voice filled my head. *Dad is demanding for me to meet with the other council members.*

Mr. Rafferty was taking Evan. He told Sherry and me that we had to come too. Unease filled my body. *I'll see you there.*

The rest of the walk was made in silence. The fact that they demanded Sherry and me as well made me nervous. Maybe they recorded our conversation in the dorm the other night. Except that Micah had been examining our dorms every day for cameras and whatnot, so there shouldn't have been anything in the room.

Kai was outside, working with Gertrude when he noticed me. His gaze flickered back to Mr. Rafferty and then came back to me with concern.

I wanted to say something to him, but right now wasn't the time.

We marched into the building, and soon we were on the top floor. When we entered the room, we found all of the other council members there along with the other three heirs and even Amber.

Why the hell was that bitch here?

Mr. Rafferty joined the council at the table while the three of us joined Liam and the others.

The seven of us faced the council members together.

Liam reached over and grabbed my hand, pulling me

beside him in the middle of the group.

Mr. Hale moved his seat so he could remain standing while the other three members followed suit. "Last night, something troubling came to a head."

This confirmed what I had thought. The rebellion hadn't told us when they planned to strike, but the timing made sense. They'd want to get out whoever they could right away.

"Oh, no. What was it?" Amber's fake voice sounded like Minnie Mouse.

Mr. Green stiffened. "Are you taking us for fools?"

"What?" Amber's face dropped, and confusion took over.

"We hadn't informed you all, but we had someone in custody at one of the headquarters, who we thought had ties to the rebellion. Last night, someone broke them out."

"Who was it?" Liam asked.

Thankfully, we didn't know much so we might be able to get out of this without lying.

"Why don't you tell them?" Mr. Croft crossed his arms as he stared Amber down.

"I was sworn to secrecy by you." Amber's voice shook, and her heart increased in pace.

"Yes, you knew." Mr. Hale pointed at her. "You also knew about another prisoner we had who was somehow rescued as well."

Holy shit. They thought she was the mole.

"Yes, but I didn't do anything." The stench of rotten eggs wafted off her. "I didn't tell anyone."

"That's bullshit." Mr. Hale slammed his hand down on the table. "Do you really think you can lie to us?"

I wanted to give him an eye roll. He always seemed to do that when he was trying to make a point.

"No, I only told Robyn. That was it." Amber lifted both hands. "She and her friends were the only ones."

Oh, wow. Those two bitches were meant for each other.

"You not only disobeyed us, but now, because of you, two important shifters who could've been spies for the rebellion have escaped our grasp." Mr. Hale gestured to the sons. "Now you will learn what to do with people who betray you."

"What? No." Amber's bottom lip quivered. "Please. I didn't know they were tied to the rebellion."

She wasn't lying. The rotten smell wasn't coming off of her anymore. "She's telling the truth." I couldn't let someone innocent get hurt, especially since it was our fault.

"This is council business, so you need to butt out." Mr. Hale yelled at the top of his lungs. "Guards!"

The door opened, and two men in black uniforms entered the room. The taller one bowed his head. "Yes?"

"Take this girl to the holding house." Mr. Hale motioned at Amber. "And then you," he said pointing at the other guard, "I need you to go find Ms. Grover and her two friends. Take them there as well."

Amber stumbled back a step as the guard approached her. "I didn't do anything. I'm sorry for telling them."

I had to do something. This wasn't right. Her only fault was whatever fucked up relationship she had with Robyn and her desperate need to be with Liam. Now, it was going to get both of them hurt if not worse.

"You can't be trusted." Mr. Rafferty spat the words.

The one guard left to find Robyn while the other walked over and grabbed Amber by the arms. "Come."

"No." Amber cried as she tried to dig her feet into the ground. "Liam, please help me. I didn't mean for anything to happen."

Even though she'd been a bitch to me, she didn't deserve this. I moved toward her when Liam's hold on my hand grew tighter.

The more you try to help, the worse it'll be. Liam's words were soft in my mind.

He knew I was struggling.

"Please, no." Tears poured down her cheeks as she was being dragged away. "Mia, help me." She begged as the guard dragged her past me. "I was only trying to do what my father told me to. Be useful to the council. I was trying to make him proud."

My heart broke even more. This wasn't right.

Do not react. Liam's voice was rough with emotion, but his face remained motionless. *If you do anything, they'll be taking you with her. That's what they want.*

But she didn't tell them. His words made sense, but it was so damn hard to stand here and watch. Maybe we could save her.

"God, please." She yelled as she was forced out the door, and when it slammed shut, an eerie silence filled the air.

"We don't tolerate mistakes." Mr. Hale adjusted his tie around his neck as a small smirk filled his face when his eyes landed on Sherry and then locked with mine. "We know you're up to something. Even though we haven't found proof, all of it will eventually come out."

He was trying to intimidate us. "I'm not up to anything." We were only doing what was right.

"Bullshit!" Mr. Rafferty yelled, and his face turned a shade of red. "We aren't stupid. You may be messing with the heirs' heads, but they will eventually fall back in line."

"In line?" I hated these four men. They were arrogant,

cruel assholes. They didn't deserve to breathe, let alone lead.

"Enough." Mr. Hale looked down his nose at us. "We will find out what you're up to. We aren't stupid, and eventually, everyone makes a mistake." He pointed to the door. "There are severe repercussions for those who don't listen to us."

"And you four." Mr. Hale turned his attention over to the heirs. "You better think carefully about what your next actions will be. Otherwise, we may be forced to retain control of the council."

"You can't do that." Liam lifted his chin in defiance.

"Oh, but we can." Mr. Green chuckled.

"Those alphas you met, they are loyal to us." Mr. Croft stood. "If we say you aren't fit to lead, they will back us."

"We're the ones in control." A smirk spread across Mr. Hale's face. "Don't force us to remind you of that. Amber is a testament to what could happen to an heir or anyone else who wants to rise against us. Let this be a warning. You're dismissed."

They were cold-hearted killers. There was no doubt in my mind that they had done something similar to my father. Any hope of them redeeming themselves was gone. They were going to pay.

The only problem that shook me was that I wasn't sure if they were passing judgment on Amber to the heirs as an example or if they were threatening us. Either way, it wasn't good.

When the six of us walked out into the hallway, her cries were already gone, and my phone buzzed in my pocket. I pulled it out, and there was another text.

Get Kai out now. The council is on to him. - W

CHAPTER TEN

We have a big problem. It wasn't like I could just tell them all right now. We had just left the council room, and there were guards all around.

What's wrong? Liam sounded tired.

I couldn't blame him. It wasn't even noon, and we had already gone through so fucking much today. *I just got another text from Willow.* I couldn't even put it into words even though the message was very simple, so I handed my phone over to him.

Fuck. He took a deep breath and gave it back to me. However, his whole demeanor hadn't changed. *Show Evan when we get on the elevator.*

He was so much better at this than I was.

The six of us got on the elevator, and it took every ounce of my self-control not to blurt out the words. Kai had just been outside the building. I only hoped he wasn't there any longer or this might get even more complicated.

I nudged Evan, who was on the other side of me, and handed him the phone with the message already lit up.

His brows furrowed for a moment before it seemed to sink in. He handed it back to me as he clenched his jaw.

Once we were out of the elevator and standing outside, I realized Kai wasn't there, like I hoped. But now I wasn't sure if I should be relieved or petrified. Did he leave on his own accord, or did the guards already get him?

It'll be fine. Liam took my hand. *There would be a huge crowd out here if they'd gotten him. The council will make sure that Amber and Robyn are taken discreetly. They don't want to upset their fathers more than they already will be. And besides, we weren't up there for that long.*

He couldn't be sure. What if they had just grabbed him and ran?

"Hey." Gertrude's voice called out from behind me. "Do you know where Kai went?"

"What?" I heard the words, but it was like I couldn't process them.

"No, weren't you with him?" Liam asked as Evan waved the others in our group away to fill them in on what was going on.

"He told me to go run a lap around the whole damn school, and when I got back here, he was gone." Gertrude rolled her eyes. "I'm so sick of this. I'm going to ask Coach Riley to train me now that Tripp is gone." She headed off toward the gym.

"Well, at least we know he wasn't taken." Liam pointed at my phone. "Text him and see if he responds."

"Okay." My hands shook as I typed out the message.

Where are you?

"What is this? Get rid of the exes in one day?" Simon headed over to the two of us. "Maybe you should consider it a blessing. One stone, two issues solved."

Sherry smacked him on the back of the head. "Dear

God. Can you not just be nice for once? This isn't something to joke over."

"Hey." Simon rubbed his head. "That hurt."

"Good." She arched an eyebrow at him.

"So, where do you think he went?" Micah scanned the perimeter like Kai was just going to stroll out from the trees.

"I'll go check the men's dorm, but I doubt he'd be there." Evan motioned at Liam and me. "The rest of you go to Sherry's dorm room. Maybe he'd show up there for help."

"But he saw us walk by this morning?" Micah sighed.

"Fine, go walk the perimeter." Evan nodded. "Simon and Sherry can start from one side and you on the other. If someone finds him, text us. Just make sure you get him off campus as soon as possible."

We all split up as four guards came barreling outside. They scanned the area, looking for someone.

I had a feeling I knew exactly who.

We had to hurry.

Slow down and don't act suspicious. Liam tugged my hand, causing me to walk at more of a leisurely pace. *They don't know his smell yet, so we have a little time.*

How do you know that? For them to be unable to sniff Kai out was a good thing.

Because the guards don't know him. Hell, Kai has probably only walked by them a handful of times. As we reached the door to the girls' dorm, Liam dropped my hand and opened the door for me. *So, hopefully, we can find him before they get on his trail.*

I tried to walk through the door calmly, but my body was pumping with adrenaline. Yeah, I hated Amber, but I would never wish something like that on her. And if Kai got captured too, well, I didn't know if I could handle it. Even though we didn't work out, he still meant something to me—my friend.

We reached the elevator, and with a shaky hand, I pressed the UP button.

Hey, it's going to be okay. He pulled me into his arms.

I don't think you can make that promise right now. However, I couldn't do anything but melt into his arms, feeling so damn ashamed that I was feeling better at the moment.

The one thing I've learned about that asshole is he has a way of getting out of things. Liam's words were laced with jealousy.

What do you mean? There were feelings of dislike between them even before I came along.

It doesn't matter right now. He dropped his arms and took my hand once more as we headed toward the open door.

We moved into the elevator, and within seconds, we were entering the dorm. The breath was knocked out of me when I saw Kai and Bree sitting on the couch.

"It's about damn time you two got here." Bree jumped to her feet and marched over to us. "We've been waiting for you."

"Whoa. We got here as soon as we could after the text." Liam's eyes began glowing with his wolf. "So, calm down."

"I told her you guys were held up with the council." Kai stood and picked up a bag from the floor. "I don't know what to do, but I've gotta get out of here."

"If we run into the woods, they'll eventually follow us if they pick up his scent." It was a damned if you don't, damned if you do situation.

"I'm going to run and get the SUV." Liam glanced at me and Kai. "You two walk like you're going to the stadium, and let Kai take the woods. I'll pick you up at the corner of the parking lot. Kai, follow the tree line to the very edge of the lot. I'll pick you up there."

"That way, my trail will stop in a dead end." Kai shook his head. "Yeah, good idea."

"Make sure your scent doesn't mix with his." Liam held my gaze. "Otherwise, they're going to know you helped him. You have to separate your scent so it ends before his."

"Text the others, and tell them to continue as normal." Liam opened the door and paused before leaving. "We have to act as normal as possible. Our fathers can't know something is out of place." He shut the door, leaving us in silence.

"I'm going with you two." Bree moved over and slipped her tennis shoes on.

"You need to stay here. I don't want you to get caught as well." It was so damn hard to protect everyone.

"Don't care. You might need back up." Bree headed to the door.

There wasn't a choice but to let her come. Otherwise, she'd wind up following and potentially getting us caught. "Let's go down the back stairwell."

"Fine." She huffed. She opened the door and glanced down the hallway. "We're good."

The three of us hurried toward the stairwell. As the door shut, the silence was deafening. I took the lead and tapped into my wolf to jump down the stairs.

When I reached the bottom, Kai and Bree were right behind me. I opened the door that led out the back and glanced around. I didn't see anyone at the moment. "Let's go."

Kai hurried into the tree line as Bree and I walked along the sidewalk behind the school. We stayed close to the building and even made a point to walk by several students who were coming in from classes.

"This is torture," Bree whined as we headed toward the parking lot.

"What are you two ladies doing?" Mr. Hale's voice called from behind us.

I had to keep my act together. I turned around and faced the horrid man. "We were taking a walk. I needed to clear my head."

"I'd think that you'd be ecstatic that Amber won't be around to harass you anymore, especially after the breakfast scene the other morning." His eyes darkened as he stared at me. "She was determined to make Liam hers still."

"How do you know about that?" My chest tightened, but I forced a look of indifference on my face.

"Oh, sweet Ms. Davis." Mr. Hale chuckled darkly. "The council has eyes and ears everywhere. Did you not think I'd be watching you?"

The unveiled threat clung in the air.

I couldn't allow my demeanor to change or allow him to think he was affecting me. "Well, then I'm surprised you didn't want to keep her around." There was only so much I could take and keep quiet. "I mean you two were on the same page for that."

"What's going on?" Bree's forehead lined as she glanced back and forth between her dad and me. "Are you talking about Amber?"

"Oh, you didn't tell her?" Mr. Hale's eyes lit with excitement. "We caught our spy."

"Amber?" Bree's mouth dropped open.

Where are you two? Liam's voice popped into my head.

Your father stopped us. The longer we stayed here, the harder it'd be.

Us?

Bree's with me. I hated that we got her involved.

I'll go grab Kai and drive around to pick you two up. Liam's voice sounded relieved. *This is a good thing. Dad won't suspect us now.*

I hadn't thought of that. *True.*

Just give me a second, and I'll pull up there.

"Yes, Amber." Mr. Hale frowned. "She was so promising, but she gave information to the eastern regional alpha's daughter, and it got leaked. We had two potential rebellion members in our grasp, and now they're gone ... all because of them."

"It could've been Robyn who told someone and not Amber." Bree's nose wrinkled, and she chewed on her bottom lip. "You might be punishing the wrong person."

"Oh, both of them will get dealt the same punishment as well as any other person when I get my hands on him." His eyes scanned the area looking for someone.

He was looking for Kai. That's why he was out here.

"But Dad, Amber wouldn't do that." Bree winced.

"She shared a secret she was entrusted with." Mr. Hale's face was set in a hard frown. "That's just as bad as being part of that rebellious movement. There will not be any mercy, not for anyone."

A car pulled up next to us in the parking lot and honked its horn.

We all turned in the direction of Liam's car.

He leaned over the passenger seat. "Are you guys coming or not?"

"Wait, don't you have class today?" Mr. Hale arched an eyebrow at Bree and tilted his head.

"Yeah, but class was canceled today." Bree shrugged her shoulders. "Something about important business. He wants us to write about some landmarks, so I've forced myself on these two."

I waited for the stench of a lie, but the air remained clear.

"Ah, yes, that makes sense." Mr. Hale paused, and his attention landed on me. "How are your parents doing?"

The words chilled me to the bone. Was he trying to insinuate something? I hadn't talked to my parents since we had left on the trip. It hadn't crossed my mind to check in with everything going on. "They're fine." I had to maintain some control.

"Good to know." He smirked and turned toward his daughter. "Make sure you don't come back too late. You all have class in the morning."

"Thanks, Daddy." Bree hugged him. "We'll be back soon."

"Liam, if anything strange happens, you better call me." Mr. Hale turned around and headed back toward the direction of the school.

Not wanting to waste another second, I jumped in the front passenger seat as Bree slid into the back.

"What the hell was that about?" That whole interaction left me worried.

"He was trying to see if we were up to anything." Liam pulled his phone from his pocket and handed it to me. "Text the guys and let them know we have him and we'll be back later."

"I never thought I'd be saying this," Kai's voice came from the backseat, "but thank you."

"Yeah, we must really love you to do this," Bree grumbled. "Shit is getting way too real."

"How the hell did you lie to him?" I just knew we were going to get caught.

"It wasn't. I do have to do that report, and I did force myself on you." Bree patted herself on the back.

She was trouble. "Should we get the others to meet us?" I typed out a message and paused.

"No, the council is growing suspicious. They need to stay back." Liam reached over and took my hand. "It'll be better that way."

"But don't you do everything together?" It might appear weird if we didn't.

"No, that was always an illusion." Liam pulled up to the gate and waved at the guard. "We're closer now than we've ever been."

"It's because you are all changing." Bree leaned forward and winked at me. "I always knew they would."

"All right, you can get up now." Liam increased the speed as we drove out onto the main road.

I grabbed my phone and pulled up the last message I got from Willow.

Cargo is in tow. Where do we meet you? - M

"Your dad asked about my parents." Those words rang in my ears. "I need to call them."

Before I could pull up their number on the phone, it dinged.

Who is with you? - W

That's interesting. Why would they care? Unless they thought we could be bringing the council with us.

Kai, Bree, Liam, and me.

My phone dinged once more.

Tell Kai to bring you home. He knows the way. Don't forget to turn off your phones. That way, you can't be tracked. - W

I stared at the words for a second. "Kai, they said you know the way home. They want you to take us there."

"Yeah, okay," Kai agreed.

My finger hovered over Mom, and I hit the green SEND button to make the call. After it rang three times, my heart dropped. She usually picks up by the third ring. Soon, I was being transferred over to her voicemail. "Something's wrong."

"What is it?" Bree asked as she leaned forward while Kai climbed into the seat right behind Liam.

"Mom always answers her phone." It sounded so stupid, but damn, it was true. "It's a running joke in our family. When Dad, Max, or I call, she always answers right away." It was one thing that I took for granted until now.

"It doesn't mean that something bad happened to them." Bree reached over the seat and patted my shoulder.

However, something felt wrong.

"Once we drop Kai off, we'll go to your parents' house." Liam squeezed my hand. "We have plenty of time to do that without dad getting suspicious."

"Let me try Max and Dad, too." I tried my phone again, and each call went to voicemail. "Something isn't right."

"Well, where you're dropping me off is along the way. Head on to Kansas City, and in about thirty minutes, we'll need to get off the interstate."

"Are you taking us there?" Bree's eyes widened.

"That's what Willow said to do." Kai shrugged his shoulders and sighed. "Believe it or not, I agree with her. It's time that the heirs and Mia see everything."

"What are you talking about?" I turned my body around and glared at Kai.

"We're heading to the rebellion headquarters." Kai gave me a sad smile. "It's time for you to be part of the planning."

"That's why she wants us to turn off our phones." I hated to do it in case Mom called back, but this was just as important. I forced myself to turn off my phone. "We should listen to them."

If I wasn't worried about my parents, I'd be excited about the opportunity. The only thing I wanted to do was to get to my family though. Something told me they weren't safe.

CHAPTER ELEVEN

W e exited from the highway and had driven at least another thirty minutes. We were now several miles from the closest town and continued passing farm after farm. "I thought you said it was on the way to checking on my parents."

I was worried sick about them. I felt even worse about it since I had to turn my phone off because even if they were trying to call me back, I wouldn't know.

"It is." He sighed. "I mean, we had to travel on the highway in that direction."

"That's not the same since we've driven just as long on this road." Bree frowned as she tapped her finger on the arm of the chair. "At least, it's kind of off the grid."

"Yeah, that's actually the point." Kai pointed to a gravel road up ahead on the left. "Turn right there."

"Okay." Liam slowed the car down and took the turn as directed. "Should we be worried that you're taking us here? This could be some kind of setup."

"No, the others have been wanting to meet Mia." Kai

shrugged his shoulders. "They are still very wary about the other heirs and hesitant about you."

"Why?" Liam glanced in the rearview mirror at Kai. "I've been with her every step of the way."

"Yeah, but that's a recent change. In the last couple of months." Kai pointed at me. "She's always been this way."

"What the hell?" Liam asked as he pounded on the steering wheel, reminding me of his father.

"Oh, stop being a drama queen." Bree rolled her eyes. "Your twenty years of past actions before Mia can't be erased in the matter of only a handful of months. Don't act stupid. You're better than that."

"She's right." I hated it for him. He had changed so much since we completed our bond, but facts were facts. He'd been an arrogant, unaware asshole before then, who would do his father's bidding. "But don't worry." I leaned over and kissed his stubbly cheek. "After spending time with you, they'll know where your heart is."

"I'm not sure about that." Liam sighed as he glanced at me out of the corner of his eye. "Kai is right."

"But they are allowing you to come with me." I squeezed his hand gently. "That means something."

It was strange. I'd expected some woods to appear, but this gravel road just took us to more flat ground.

"There is something you should know before we get there." Kai blew out a breath. "It's only fair that I tell you two after you just saved my ass."

Sentences like that never end with anything good.

"Unless you've already told them." Kai turned his head in Bree's direction.

"I have no clue what you're talking about." Bree's brows furrowed.

"Well, okay then." Kai shrugged his shoulders. "I guess it

makes sense that they would leave that piece out for you as well."

"Get to the point." Liam slowed to a stop. "Or I'll make you."

"Oh, there's the Liam I grew up with." Kai chuckled as he shook his head. "Okay. So when the rebellion first started, the whole intent was to be heard."

"Wait." I wasn't sure why I hadn't asked this question to begin with. "How long has the rebellion group been around?"

"Ever since Brent Forrest died." Kai bit his lip and cleared his throat. "It started out small. For the Overseer to die, it was a huge deal. The rest of the council members should've stepped down, but there was no one there to take over. Hell, we were all only two years old." Kai glanced at Liam.

"But why didn't we hear about it while growing up?" Liam asked.

"Because your parents were ignoring it." He scanned the road. "They are watching us, so we have to be quick. They'll be able to fill you in better than me. But their plan was to disband the council."

"What do you mean disband?" Bree scratched the back of her neck.

"It's pretty fucking obvious what he means," Liam growled. "We don't need to disband. We need our dads to step down."

"At one point, I would've said I didn't agree with you, but..." Kai took in a deep breath and met Liam's eyes. "I agree with you now. At first, I thought it was something you were only doing to make things right with Mia and that it wouldn't last. But it has. She's changed you."

"No, I didn't change him." That's what the council

thought, and it was why they wanted the heirs to turn away from their fated mates like they'd done theirs. However, the truth was something they couldn't grasp. "I only grounded him."

"That actually makes sense." Bree nodded. "Because he's more like the Liam we grew up with, and hell, Sherry sure has made a change in Simon."

"I'm not sure if that's still their plan now, but I wanted you to at least know what the original intent was." Kai nodded in the direction of the road. "Now, we need to go before they get suspicious."

"All right." Liam pressed the gas again. "Thanks."

The rest of the trip passed in silence. Right when I was about to give up on us ever getting there, the gravel road disappeared into a dirt one, and I saw several houses up ahead.

A line of about ten people stood in front of us, effectively cutting the road off from entering the small neighborhood. Willow was the one directly in the middle and it took me a second to comprehend the person standing right next to her, staring us down.

"Your father is part of the rebellion?" I wasn't sure if I spoke the words loud enough for him to hear.

"Yes, that's who they broke out in Chicago and why I was in danger." Kai blew out a breath and straightened his shoulders.

"That makes sense now." Bree pursed her lips. "But why are they blocking us from entering?"

"They want to scan my car and make sure we aren't hiding something or someone in here." Liam put the car in PARK and glanced at me. *You stay beside me at all times.*

No problem on that one. I wouldn't let him out of my

sight either. We were a package deal, and they were going to have to see that.

The four of us climbed out of the car, and Mr. Thorn sagged with relief.

It was strange because it appeared as if he had aged ten years since I'd last seen him not even two weeks ago.

"I was so worried." Mr. Thorn sighed.

Kai hurried past us, went to his dad, and hugged him.

Bree, Liam, and I stayed next to the car. I wasn't moving away from our only way out if things went south.

"Anyone else in there?" Willow moved in our direction with two men flanking each side of her.

She wanted to get close enough to be able to smell if we lied. I couldn't blame her though.

I waited until she was only a few feet away. Liam stepped in front of both Bree and me, leaving only half of us visible to the rebellion.

"You know I already answered that." I had to make sure she knew I wouldn't be pushed around.

"Can you humor me?" She arched an eyebrow as she stepped to her right in order to see me entirely. "Please?"

"Fine, I told you that it was only the four of us." I pointed to Kai, Bree, Liam, and then me. "The story hasn't changed."

"Go check the vehicle." Willow motioned to the guard to her left.

The guy pulled out some large instrument, walked over to the driver's side, and opened the back door. He climbed into the vehicle and searched, using the machine.

I get that they needed to be careful, but at this point, we'd proven to be at least somewhat on their team.

It only took a second before the guy jumped out. "All clear."

She took a deep breath, and then a smile spread across her face. "Well, okay then." She nodded to the subdivision. "Let's go meet some people and talk."

"I'm sorry, but we can't stay." I hadn't been able to get the nagging feeling about my family to go away. I'd been so stupid not to even consider that the council would try to use them against me. They had already used Max.

"Why not?" She shifted her weight to one side.

"I need to check on my parents." I had nothing to lose by being honest with her. "Something was said that alluded to their well-being."

"Then you've come to the right place." She turned around and looked at the other guys. "I'm good with it if Milo is." She nodded her head to Kai's father.

Milo? I linked with Liam as I watched her address Mr. Thorn.

That's Kai's Dad's first name. Liam took my hand in his and pulled me close to his side.

"Yeah, it's fine." Mr. Thorn nodded at me. "She's trustworthy."

"Fine, but what about those two?" The tallest guy next to Willow raised his hand to point in Liam and Bree's direction. His long, black hair was pulled into a low ponytail, and with the movement of his arm, his shirt rose just enough to get a glimpse of rock hard abs. He couldn't be much older than us, yet his eyes seemed so mature.

"They're fine." Willow turned toward the guy who was at least five inches taller than her. "I won't repeat myself again."

"Damn. Fine." The guy turned on his heel and marched off toward the houses.

"Ignore him." Willow winked at me. "He's kind of anal. Now let's go."

The group all turned their backs to us, heading in the same direction.

"Wait, we've got to go." I just told her I needed to get home.

"You'll want to see this before you leave." Mr. Thorn stopped and glanced over his shoulder. "I promise."

"If you want to go, we can just leave." Liam pulled me into his arms. "We don't have to listen to them."

"I agree with Liam." Bree reached over and touched my arm.

"Let's see what they want to show us first." The rebellion was offering a peek into how they operated. I'd be stupid to reject this offer. I might need their help to free my parents. "Then we'll go."

Are you sure? Liam's voice was rough with concern.

Yes, but I don't want to stay long. I stood on my tiptoes and kissed his cheek.

"Do we leave your car here?" Bree glanced around.

"Yeah, they didn't mention for me to bring it in. It's not like we're far anyway." Liam released me from his arms and took my hand in his. "Let's get in and out."

"Sounds good to me." Bree stepped over to my other side and we followed the others.

When we caught back up with them, they stopped where the road split into a huge circle. Everyone except Willow, Kai, and Mr. Thorn went to the left while the three of them waited for us.

"We have a surprise for you." Mr. Thorn smiled as he pointed over to the fourth house on the right. "Why don't you go knock on that door?"

That was a strange request but one I was willing to oblige. "Okay."

I don't like this. Liam's body tensed next to mine.

They can't risk losing our help. We were an asset to them right now. *It'll be fine.*

Bree stayed on my other side, and we quickly approached the house. The houses were small and modest, but they seemed solidly built. They were all painted white and looked exactly the same. When I reached the door, I held my hand out and knocked on it.

The door opened in seconds, and what I saw stole my breath.

"Mia." Mom's mouth dropped open, and she paused for a second before pulling me into her arms.

I wrapped my arms around her, taking in a breath of her chocolate scent.

"I've been so worried about you." She yelled over her shoulder. "Ethan! Max! She's here!"

"What?" I heard my father's familiar, deep voice call from inside.

"All three of you are here?" All the stress that had been bottled up inside me calmed.

"Yes, we are." She let me go and then pulled Liam into a huge hug. "We were worried about both of you."

Liam's body tensed for a second before he relaxed and returned my mother's warm embrace.

"You can't hog them all to yourself." Ethan slid past mom, who was blocking the doorway, and pulled me into a bone-crushing hug.

I hugged him back, my heart so full it felt like it might explode. "How did you guys get here?"

"Well, someone showed up at our door while you were away on that trip and told me that we needed to come with them." Dad let me go. "At first, we were hesitant, but we already knew what the council had done to Max. We couldn't chance that again."

At the sound of his name, he came out onto the front porch and winked at me. "Hey, sis." He and Ethan were the spitting image of each other. They had light blond hair and dark eyes that looked as if they could see into your soul.

"And Bree. Long time no see." He gave me a side hug and then walked over to her.

"Bree?" Mom focused more on my friend.

"Oh, this is Liam's sister, Bree." I took her hand, pulling her in my direction. "She's the one who got me accepted into Wolf Moon."

"It's nice to meet you all." She gave them a warm smile and shook their hands.

"Wait, if you're here, does that mean you got pulled out of KSU?" I hadn't even considered that until this moment.

"For now. When this is all over, I'll go back." Max winked at me.

This was all my fault. They were in hiding because of me. "I'm so sorry guys."

"No, don't you dare." Mom lifted her chin. "I was wrong about it all. I should've told you from the very beginning who you were. I didn't realize how important you were to our packs."

"But I'm not. I'm making everything worse." Ever since I got accepted into Wolf Moon, it'd been one thing after another. "Now you have to hide here, and Max had to leave school."

"You are making a difference." Mom then pointed at Liam and Bree. "You all are bringing the issues that all of our packs are facing to light. Something that's needed to be done ever since your father didn't return to me."

"She's right." Liam's eyes filled with adoration. "You're the Overseer. The one who fate created to level out the council. This change couldn't have gotten this far without you."

"And on that note." Mr. Thorn's voice came from behind. "I'd like to talk to the three of them alone for a few minutes before they have to go."

I gave them another huge hug. "I'm sorry, but we do need to talk to him. We'll come back as soon as we can to visit with you all again."

"I love you, honey." Mom hugged me once more while Dad wrapped his arms around both of us.

"Bye." Liam nodded at them, and the three of us turned and made our way back to Mr. Thorn.

"Let's go someplace we can talk." He pointed to a building that was slightly larger than the rest of them.

When we entered the building, we discovered it was one huge room with a rectangle wooden table in the center. Willow and Kai were already sitting there together on one side.

"We'd like to discuss a few things before you head back." Mr. Thorn sat beside Kai.

I took the middle seat directly across from Kai with Liam on my right and Bree to my left.

"First off, thank you for saving my parents. I was afraid that I might've been too late." The fact that they did that when they didn't have to spoke volumes to me.

"Yeah, you would've been." Willow tilted her head.

"Well, if you hadn't gotten my son when you did, he wouldn't be sitting here beside me." Mr. Thorn reached over and patted Kai on the shoulder. "So, we're even there."

"Yeah, thank you." Kai placed his hands on the table.

"You're our friend." Bree shook her head. "You don't have to thank us."

"So what is the point of us being here?" Liam dropped

his hands into his lap. "Kai told us you were the one who was broken out from Chicago headquarters."

"Yes, it was me." Mr. Thorn nodded.

"How long have you been a part of this?" It was still kind of hard to believe, especially after the first time I had met him. He had appeared so calculating just like the council members.

"Ever since your father passed away." Mr. Thorn met my eyes as though in challenge.

Now, I had to face my hidden bloodline. There was no going back.

CHAPTER TWELVE

"Wait..." Kai turned his head in his father's direction. "Her father is alive."

"You don't already know?" I'd figured if Willow knew, everyone else here did as well.

"No, we couldn't risk him giving up that information if the council caught on to us." Willow tilted her head in my direction and arched an eyebrow. "Now he won't be going back, so it isn't as risky."

"Then, why are we here?" Liam leaned back in his seat and studied Mr. Thorn.

"Because you and the rest of your group need to get acclimated to the rebellion." Mr. Thorn took a deep breath. "But if you left, your fathers would grow suspicious. We need them thinking you're on their side. With your group, we have to risk it all."

"Why? You could just attack them on campus." That was one place where they were all together. It was the main meeting grounds for all four regions to come together.

"All the other regional, district, and city alphas are loyal to them." Willow lifted her feet and put her shoes on the table, sprawling out. "So even if we did take the council members out, we'd still be facing a war across the regions. They'd force their alpha will on the packs, and we'd be destroyed."

"This has always been our problem." Mr. Thorn blew out a breath. "Until you." He focused on me.

"Wait, I thought you wanted to take the council down." Kai pointed at Liam.

"Yes, that was our goal originally, but now it might not have to be." Mr. Thorn motioned in my direction.

"Hold on." Willow dropped her feet back on the ground and stood, facing him. "We haven't discussed this, and I'm not sure if I'm on board."

"You want us to take the council seats." Liam pulled my hand into his. "If you wait another six months to a year, it'll happen."

"Will it?" Willow focused on him. "You think your loving parents are going to hand it over to you?"

Don't tell them anything. Liam squeezed my hand. *They may have started trusting us, but they haven't done anything to prove their loyalty to us.*

"It's the law." Bree's forehead creased.

"It's also law that they are supposed to take care of their people." Willow sneered. "And they aren't holding up to that either."

She had a point there, and Bree didn't know what they'd threatened us with only a few hours ago. I was on the same page as the rebellion. The members didn't plan on giving up their seats ... at least not willingly.

"All of them are changing." Kai's words were soft but stern. "Even Simon, which is crazy."

"I saw it too." Mr. Thorn pointed at Liam. "If we have

the heirs on our side, the other alphas won't have much to argue about."

"It could still be a civil war even with them." Willow sat back in the chair, but her body was still stiff.

"If we can start helping the struggling packs, they would pledge their loyalty to us over the council members." They needed to see a set of heirs who truly cared like they had when the first original council was established. "Get our message out to them all, and let them know that the heirs stand behind this movement."

"But that sounds ridiculous..." Willow rolled her eyes.

"No, it makes perfect sense." Liam scooted closer to me. "Essentially, they would view us as the alphas and not our parents. They would pledge their loyalty to us."

"Yes, and with the information that the Overseer is taking the lead, they wouldn't be afraid to stand behind a complete council." Mr. Thorn smiled at Liam.

"But how do we accomplish all of that and keep it from their parents?" This would be risky. However, there honestly wasn't another alternative at this point.

"Maybe you create a new seal as your representation and let the rebellion know you need more followers before you can take down the current council. That if they let out your names, their life can't ever change for the better." Kai glanced at his dad and then Willow. "Everyone who hears the message will be those who would do absolutely anything to get out of their life situation, including keeping the information secret."

"A symbol replacing their names would help prevent the heirs' names from being spread everywhere to deliver the message." Bree shrugged her shoulders.

"It's nice being part of meetings like these and not

having to bear any of the risks and responsibilities." Liam's eyes darkened as he stared Kai down.

I had always thought it was odd how the two of them hated each other. Although it was growing more and more clear that this was something that had happened years ago before I got here. I needed to talk to Liam about it later.

"If we're going to do this, we need to be strategic. We have to prove to them that the heirs have really changed." We were front and center, yet not front and center. "How many people live here?"

"We have about two hundred scattered around." Mr. Thorn motioned out the door. "We are continually building more homes with bare minimum needs. If people come here, it's because they somehow got free or are in need of protection. We don't turn anyone away."

"Do you have room for more?" The more people we had here, the more we could control the message and reduce our risk of being found out.

"Yes, houses can be built by our pack in a week or two." Willow pointed to the door. "That's how we all kind of earn our keep. More and more show up every day whether it's from us breaking a pack free or us finding them living homeless on the roads or streets."

"How much land do you have?" Liam fidgeted in his seat. "And who owns it?"

"We have over fifty acres. It's owned by a human, not a shifter." Mr. Thorn gave a sad smile. "He's one of my best friends growing up. Since he's human, we didn't hang out in public much, but we grew close over the years. His wife died around the same time mine did, which brought us closer. I kept him apart from the shifter life up until now."

I felt like an asshole. I hadn't even known Kai's mom was dead. "At least, it won't be easy to find the location."

"Do these people know how to fight?" Liam's jaw twitched, which was the only sign to me that he was even remotely concerned. "Because our parents aren't going to go down without one."

"I'd hoped it could be done a different way, but I do agree with you." Mr. Thorn took a deep breath. "Willow and her direct pack know how to fight, so I'd say that's around twenty total."

"So we need to train the rest." That was the only way we were going to make it out alive.

"It's easier said than done," Willow growled. "If it was that easy, we'd be the ones training them, but we go on the missions. If we need to save someone or intervene, it's me and my men who handle it. And unfortunately, that number is increasing every day, so we don't have the time or the luxury to train anyone."

"That's something the heirs can do." All four of them were amazing fighters and grew up needing to defend themselves. And hell, Evan alone was a force to be reckoned with.

"Yeah." Liam glanced at me and smiled. "That way, we have a face with the people who are here and don't risk getting caught in the crossfire. They can focus on the mission, and our group can train the ones left behind."

"I could even help too." Kai lifted a hand. "If that's cool with you guys."

"Are you going to be easy on them like you were Mia?" Liam lifted his chin.

Kai took in a deep breath. "Look, she's different..."

"We've made it very clear how different she is to you." Liam's voice was low and raspy but, surprisingly, not a growl.

"That's enough." I punched Liam in the arm. "That's all

in the past. Evan is an amazing trainer, so I'm sure he can accomplish leaps and bounds with them."

"Wait... Are you talking about all the heirs coming here?" Willow arched an eyebrow and shook her head no. "No way in hell."

"Uh... yeah." Bree snorted. "What did you expect?"

"We're a team." Even if it was a recent development, we were a package deal. "You accept all of us or none of us."

"They're welcome here." Mr. Thorn looked at me. "It won't be an issue."

"Milo!" Willow snapped her head in his direction. "We're taking a risk..."

"It's already done." Mr. Thorn pointed at the three of us sitting across from them. "They're here, and she's right; they're a package deal. She and Liam aren't the only ones ascending the council. All five of them are."

"Still, it would've been nice to have a word before you made a decision like that. It affects us all, not just you and your son." Willow's face had turned almost the same shade as her hair. "This isn't even your region."

"Actually, it is." Mr. Thorn closed his eyes and crossed his arms. "We are here because of my contact. Also, I was the one who found and recruited you. They're welcome because with them, we might have a chance to win this damn war." He opened his eyes and locked gazes with her.

An awkward silence descended around us as the two stared each other down. It was a battle of wills.

Sweat sprouted above Willow's lip as her wolf submitted to Mr. Thorn. Soon, her body started shaking, and she averted her eyes to the ground.

"Dammit." She growled the words.

"We better head back." Bree stood and took a deep breath. "It's getting late."

"She's right." Liam followed her lead. *Let's get out of here.*

"We'll make a schedule and send it to you shortly. Considering the way the council is watching us, all of us can't be gone at one time right now." A chill ran down my spine as I remembered the words Mr. Hale had spoken only a few hours ago. "So, I'll give you an update when we have it coordinated."

"Let me walk you three out." Kai jumped to his feet, eager to get out from between the unhappy pair.

The four of us stepped out of the building, and the sun was already setting in the sky. We'd been out here longer than I thought.

"You all be careful heading back." Kai stopped moving and saluted us. "I owe you guys one since you saved my ass when you didn't have to."

"Let's just call it even since you helped us find Mia that one time." Liam's voice grew oddly quiet at the end.

"Yeah, okay." Kai nodded at Liam and sighed. "All right, I guess we'll be seeing you soon."

"Come on. We need to get back." Liam tugged me toward his Escalade.

"See you," Bree called over her shoulder as the three of us made it back to our car.

When we all got situated, Liam turned the car around, and we headed back to the main road.

"We need to roll the windows down to get his scent out of here," Bree said as she rolled down her windows.

"No one is getting in this car besides us." Liam glanced in the rearview mirror. "Isn't that kind of overkill?"

"Better safe than sorry though." I had to agree with Bree on this one. "We don't want your dad to do a search or something when we get back on campus. They're going to know Kai escaped by a vehicle somehow."

"Fine." Liam rolled down his window, and silence filled the car.

WHEN WE PULLED BACK on to the interstate, the air whipping through the car was the only noise. *Hey, let's roll the windows up.* Even though we didn't want Kai's smell to be in the car, we surely didn't want to make it where our smells weren't either.

Liam pressed the button, sealing off the vehicle again with silence.

"We need to turn on the phones." We needed them to think something odd happened while we were gone and where we lost signal was near where we appeared back on the grid. We always did it at the exact same place, a bar in Kansas City, so if they came to check it out, they'd think we'd been hanging out there.

"Okay," Bree said as the sounds of her taking her phone apart hit my ears. "These smart devices are a pain in the ass when it comes to the battery."

She wasn't kidding there. I grabbed both my and Liam's phones and went to work on them.

When we finally pulled into school and back into Liam's parking spot, I wasn't surprised to see Mr. Hale standing there, waiting on us.

As we stepped from the car, he arched an eyebrow. "You three have been gone a while."

"Yeah, we lost track of time." Liam grinned as he nodded at his father. "What are you doing out here so late?"

"We have an issue that we're trying to deal with." His face turned into a frown.

"Anything we can help you with?" Bree's smile was so sincere it shocked me.

"No, it's nothing for you three to worry about."

Mr. Rafferty stood in the grassy field between the dorm and restaurant. "Jacob, we need you back in the council room."

"On my way." Mr. Hale scanned the three of us once more before nodding at us. "I have business to attend to, but I'll see you soon." He turned and headed toward Mr. Rafferty.

The three of us began our trek to the dorms.

"Do we want everyone to meet up here?" Bree asked as she pointed to the girls' dorm.

"No, we don't need to have a meeting right now. They're keeping tabs on us, and it might stir questions if we all got together." Liam wet his lips as he took my arm and tugged me toward his room. "We'll meet in the morning."

"Got it." Bree gave me a quick side hug. "See you tomorrow."

Do you think he was suspicious of us? His father hadn't asked any leading questions, which sort of surprised me.

No, he's going to get the spare key to my car and check it out. Liam held open the front door to the men's dorm room.

Well, it's a good thing we followed Bree's advice. There shouldn't be any evidence of Kai in there now.

Yeah, she knows how he thinks too.

So are you upset that he's going to search your car? That was a huge invasion of privacy.

Yeah, but I can't do anything about it. Liam frowned as he stepped into the elevator. *The car may be mine, but it was purchased with our family money. It is what it is.*

Within minutes, we were walking into his dorm room, and it was silent.

"Evan?" Liam called out, but there was no response.

"He must be helping them or something." Liam pulled me into his arms and kissed my forehead. "It feels as if this whole thing is never-ending."

As I melted in his arms, I had to agree. "It's got to get better at some point."

He lowered his lips to mine and sighed. *This always makes me feel better.*

It felt like it'd been weeks since we'd spent any time together like this, but it had only been a matter of days. *Yeah, it does feel pretty great.* I deepened the kiss, needing to feel his touch all around me.

His hands traveled down my waist to my ass. He groaned as he pulled my body flush against him, and I felt his hardness.

A low moan escaped me as I wrapped my arms around his neck. *I love you.*

I love you too. He picked me up by my waist and headed to his bedroom. As we entered the room, he slammed the door behind him. He placed me gently on his king-size bed and never once separated his lips from mine.

His fingers unbuttoned my jeans, and his hands slipped inside to touch me.

That feels so good. His touches always made me so dizzy. I wanted him to know how he made me feel.

With his free hand, he tugged my shirt upward. I broke our kiss to pull it over my head and toss it to the floor. He reached around me and unfastened my bra in one swift move. I layback, relishing the feel of his body all over me.

My hands jerked as I pulled on his shirt, needing to feel his body against mine with no barriers. He growled as he lifted back up and yanked down my pants and underwear before removing and throwing his own clothes on the floor.

He kissed down my neck as his fingers found my most sensitive spot below again. He kissed my breast as I blindly reached out and felt his length in my hand.

Right when he was about to pleasure my body, I yanked his hand away and wrapped my legs around his waist. *Enough.*

Thank God. He said those words as he rocked inside me, and the feel of him had me coming unglued. We moved together as one for minutes or hours. I wasn't sure, but I wouldn't change it for the world.

Soon, he sped up as the pleasure built inside both of us. We both needed the release, and when it poured through our bodies, we both moaned in pleasure.

He rolled to the side and pulled me against his chest. *Tonight, let's focus on you and me. We need a break from this world.*

That sounds perfect to me. I cuddled against him and tried to enjoy the moment. Tomorrow, we had hard decisions to make.

CHAPTER THIRTEEN

The next few days passed in a blur. The rumor mill was going wild with Amber, Tripp, Kai, Robyn, and her two friends disappearing without a trace. A scandal like this hadn't happened for years.

We'd planned on taking the others to the rebellion. Having our group meet everyone and begin training, but we were being watched like a hawk tracking its prey. We figured, at least the first time, the whole group should be present, but that couldn't be a habit. Eyes were on us at all times, so we had to be careful. Luckily, we were able to communicate with them via the burner phone. I wasn't even willing to risk calling from my personal phone any longer.

It was Saturday, and the guys had another football game offsite. One that was hosted by a below-average college and far enough away that we'd have to stay overnight. It worked in our favor.

Liam had been called bright and early this morning by his father, informing him that he and the other council members wouldn't be able to make it to the game. Something about the possibility of them finally catching a break in their mole problem.

At first, we'd all been suspicious, but most of the guards had left with them. Mr. Thorn had comforted us several times, telling us they were chasing a ghost, so there were no worries on our end.

Liam had informed the coach that they were driving separately. The coach hadn't been thrilled, but what could he do. They were the heirs after all. Others still saw that as a big deal even though we were all well aware that their fathers didn't intend to hand things over.

Bree and Sherry sat beside me in the student section, and despite it being an away game, the bleachers were half-filled. Most of them were from surrounding wolf packs who wanted to support their future leaders.

As usual, Liam and the others on the field were dominating the other team. It didn't appear that the host team had one wolf shifter playing for them. We were in the final quarter when the coach called the heirs to the sidelines to let the more inexperienced team members out to play.

Hey, we're in the locker room, changing. Liam linked with me. *Go on and head back to the car. We will meet you there.*

"This wasn't even a game." Bree rolled her eyes. "It was more of a killing."

"Ain't that the truth?" Sherry snorted and shook her head. "But I still enjoyed watching Simon, especially when he leaned over."

"Oh, my God. Ew!" Bree closed her eyes and stuck her fingers into her ears.

"Well, you've been enjoying this game then. The offense has been the one playing the most." I couldn't help the laugh that fell from my mouth. Bree grew up with all four of them, so she thought of them more as her brothers than anything else. "I can safely say I've thoroughly..."

"Stop right there." Bree jerked her head in my direction and pointed at me. "It's bad enough hearing her say that about Simon, but hearing you say something similar about my actual flesh and blood will make me vomit. And I'll be aiming at your shoes if I do."

She had a flair for the dramatics. I didn't realize how much I missed her until this moment. Now that I was living with Liam... and Evan, I didn't get to spend time with either Bree or Sherry very often. "Hey, I thought you were happy I mated with your brother."

"Oh, I am." She knocked her shoulder into mine. "But I still don't want to hear anything that would make him sound like more than a brother in my mind. You got it?"

I thought about my own brother. If someone was saying stuff about him, I'd probably feel the same way. "Got it."

"Hey, we need to sneak out." I tried not to glance over my shoulder, which could alert the guards, but we needed to get out of here without them noticing. "The guys are already changing."

A group of girls stood up in front of us. It was our best chance.

The three of us stood on our feet and followed the group of girls who were climbing the stairs to leave. I bumped in between the eight of them and held out my hand to one. "I'm so sorry." Instead of moving out of the way so they could all walk together, Sherry and Bree jumped in next to us.

The ones in the back rolled their eyes, but one of them seemed to recognize Bree. The observant one poked her friends in the side. "It's one of the councilmen's daughters."

"Oh... shit." They stopped in their tracks, motioning for us to keep going.

A larger group of people merged with us the closer we got to the top. I turned around and almost lifted my hands in victory when I saw the guards were still in their place, scanning for us. Our scent was lost in the sea of people.

The three of us reached the main floor, and we took off toward the doors. I tried walking slow enough to not alert any of the humans, but it was so damn hard. We reached the glass doors, and I swung them open as Bree and Sherry pushed through.

I glanced over my shoulder and grinned at the mass exodus that was taking place. As long as they didn't follow the guys, we were in good shape. We were lucky that the council members weren't here or we wouldn't have been able to pull it off, given how closely they were making the guards watch us.

The guys had parked at least three miles away, so it would be harder to locate us. They would expect us to use a paid garage close by.

The scent of shifters dissipated as we followed more of the college students toward the dorms here. It had probably worked even more in our favor to park over there.

"Hey, there." A guy touched my arm as he caught up to me. "Would you and your friends like to go to a party with us?" The guy was cute, but he had the douche look down pat.

"Nope." The less we interacted with anyone, the better.

"Oh, come on." His cold eyes scanned me from top to bottom. "It's the best party going on. Most people would die for an invite."

"Not interested." I hated men who couldn't get a clue. Hell, calling him a man was an overstatement since he obviously had the impulse control of a pre-pubescent teenage boy.

Bree tilted her head downward with her eyes raised in front of us. She wanted us to lose the creep, so the three of us sped up, leaving the guy behind.

"Hey!" I heard him call out, but if he hadn't gotten the hint before, he should have definitely figured it out by now. There was no way I was going to engage with him anymore.

After a few minutes, we spotted Liam and Evan's cars. They'd parked on the side of the road so we could easily jump in and move out.

We headed over to the cars. I pulled out the extra set of keys and unlocked the door. It'd be better if we hid inside before we drew any other unwanted attention.

Right as I reached the passenger door, someone grabbed my hand and turned me away from the car. It was the asshole again.

"I said come to the party with us." His eyes flared as I noticed his two buddies standing behind him.

"And I said no." My wolf surged forward inside me.

"Holy shit, her eyes are glowing." One of the guys behind him said. "That's freaking hot."

"It has to be the moon or something." The other guy said as he took a step back.

That was the thing about humans. They always tried to justify anything paranormal they might have seen. Granted, I had instantly pulled my wolf in enough to dissipate the glow from my eyes. She hadn't taken over completely; we knew the laws.

"Look, we're trying to be nice here." He lifted his hands outward. "We just want to get you a drink, and then you can be on your way."

"You seem to have a problem with the word no." Sherry came over and stood beside me.

"Hey, I just said we're trying to be nice," the guy who had been harassing me said as he took a step toward me. He reached out to grab my arm, and I easily side-stepped, making him catch air.

"This is your last chance before I turn mean." He breathed hard as he locked eyes with me.

"Get away from her … Now!" Liam's deep voice came from a few feet away.

All four of the heirs approached us, and Liam and Evan turned, standing next to me and facing the assholes down.

"Is she sleeping with both of you?" The guy smirked.

Liam reared back and punched the guy right in the face, and we heard a sickening crunching sound.

"Aw, shit! My nose." The guy held his nose as blood poured down his shirt and onto the pavement.

Liam turned to move, but I grabbed his arm. "We don't need to make a scene, and he's not worth it."

He paused, not wanting to go.

"She's right, man. Let's go." Evan spun on his heel and headed to his car with Micah following behind him.

I tugged on his arm once more. "Come on."

He relented as he watched the guy cradle his nose.

The rest of us climbed into Liam's car, and Liam squealed the wheels as he pulled out.

"Hey, dumbass," Simon called from the backseat where he was next to Sherry. "We're supposed to be staying under the radar."

"Oh, bite me," he growled. "If you saw someone doing that to Sherry, you would've lost control."

"Damn right I would." He lowered his head and kissed a smiling Sherry on the lips.

Bree leaned forward and turned her head to me. "It's so weird seeing him like that."

I had to agree with her. Simon had changed so much, but he was still a loose cannon. I didn't think that would ever change.

We pulled up to the rebellion headquarters around ten that night. Bree had used the phone they'd given her to call when we turned down the road close to the area. Max, Nate, Tripp, and Kai were standing at the entrance, waiting on us.

"When did Nate get here?" I asked as I opened the door.

"Oh, the rebellion helped their family escape. It appears Dad got wind of their involvement." A smile spread across her face. "So I get to spend the night with him."

"Well, I'm sure he's as excited as you." I gave her a side hug as we closed the distance to them.

"Are you guys the welcoming committee?" I went to Max and wrapped my arms around him.

The trunks closed, and soon the heirs joined our group with our overnight bags.

Liam handed Bree's over to Nate. "This one is Bree's."

"What?" Nate stood there a second before it sank in.

"Isn't she staying with you?" Liam tilted his head.

"Oh, yeah." Nate nodded his head while his body tensed with unease. "She can stay with Max and me."

"We have three units set up for the rest of you." Kai gave me a quick hug and then took a step back.

"Yours is closest to me." Tripp nudged me in the side.

"So no loud moans tonight 'cause I don't want to think of you that way."

A low growl rattled from Liam.

"Dude, I said I didn't want to." Tripp stumbled back with both hands in the air.

"Come on." Max waved us toward the houses. "We all need our rest, especially since we're waking up at six in the morning to train with everyone."

Liam took my hand as all of us headed toward the back of the subdivision.

When we reached one of the last rows of houses, Kai stopped at the first one and opened it. "This one's for Liam and Mia."

"Okay, great." I yawned. "We'll see you all in the morning."

When I walked into the little house, I stepped directly into the living room that connected with the kitchen. There was a loveseat against the wall, and the kitchen contained a wooden table.

I turned down the short hallway where a bedroom sat on the right and a bathroom with a stand-up shower to the left.

A queen bed took up almost the entire bedroom with a tiny closet that was hidden when the room's door was open.

"I'm going to take a quick shower and get to bed." Liam dropped our bag against the limited section between the wall and bed. "Go ahead and get some rest if you want to."

"Okay." I turned around and wrapped my arms around his neck. "Don't take too long."

"I won't." He leaned down and kissed my lips before he turned and headed into the bathroom.

I almost lost it when I saw him try to fit in the bathroom.

He was able to just barely, but if it had been any smaller, it could've been bad.

Not wanting to waste another second, I crawled into the bed and got settled. I fell asleep before he even got out of the shower.

———

"You ready?" Liam glanced back into the tiny bedroom. The mattress was not the most comfortable, but at least we had a roof over our heads.

"Yeah, let's go do this." I pulled my shirt down in place, finally dressed to start the day.

We walked outside and found the others waiting. Simon had dark circles under his eyes, and he was frowning.

"What's wrong with you?" He looked like he hadn't slept any last night, but he didn't have the afterglow or the smell of sex on him.

"Princess here couldn't sleep on such an uncomfortable mattress." Sherry rolled her eyes.

"Hey, I told you to stop calling me that," Simon growled.

"I don't know, man." Micah chuckled. "Princess seems pretty fitting."

"Shut the fuck up." Simon glared at his friend.

"And if I don't." Micah took a few steps in his direction.

"Oh, for the love of God." Bree rolled her eyes as she stepped out of the house with Nate. "I can hear you two bickering all the way inside the house."

"They sound like an old married couple." Liam sighed. "Can we at least pretend we have our act together?"

"Those two are impulsive." Evan walked over and hit Micah on the back of the head. "And you are instigating, so stop it."

"Ow, dammit!" Micah rubbed his head. "You know it's sensitive."

"These are the four idiots who are going to train everyone?" Willow's words dripped with sarcasm as she and Mr. Thorn walked over to us.

"Watch it, Red," Evan growled as his grey eyes took on a glow.

I wasn't sure if there was anger or lust behind them.

"They'll be fine." Mr. Thorn smiled as he took our group in. "The others are getting ready for training." He pointed to a group of people gathering in a large section of grass that was several rows of houses behind us. "We have everyone under the age of fifty there to train. The older ones are too weak."

"We need to get a move on since we have to get back on campus at a decent hour." Evan surveyed our group. "You guys ready?"

"Yeah." Simon yawned. "Let's do this so I can get back to my bed."

"I'm taking my crew out for another survey." Willow gestured in the direction of a few motorcycles. "We need to make sure they aren't on to any of the other families in that area."

"They shouldn't be." Nate frowned. "We all made sure to keep our distance from each other for plausibility, but thanks for going to check."

"That's our job." Willow sneered. "You all better make sure you get their asses ready to fight." She spun around and marched over to the five motorcycles where four of her guys were waiting for her.

Evan watched her for a second before he took a deep breath and pointed to the group of fifty. "Let's start with this group."

Mr. Thorn stayed with us, and when we reached the group, their attention locked on him.

"These are the four heirs who are here to train you." He pointed at each one. "You listen to them. They are allies to us. Now, we must prepare for war."

Max jogged over to us. "Hey, you."

"Hey." I moved over and joined the line with the other people.

"What are you doing?" Liam's brows furrowed.

"I need more training." If he thought I wasn't going to be part of the fight, then he didn't know me at all.

"Hell yeah." Sherry stood next to me. "I'm down too."

"Ugh, fine." Bree joined us. "I guess I better learn as well."

"All right, we're going to split up into four groups." Evan didn't miss a beat. "Let's split into groups of thirteen."

The group separated evenly with Sherry, Bree, Nate, Max, and me in the same group with eight other people who I didn't know. They were all about the same age as us.

"All right, I'll take this group." Evan pointed in our direction.

"No, I want that group." Liam stepped in between me and Evan.

"You can't train this one with your sister and Mia being in it." Evan nodded over to the others. "You won't do what needs to be done, and you know it. You want them to be able to protect themselves if it comes down to it, right?"

"Fine." Liam took my hand and pulled me into his arms. *If you need me, you know what to do.*

A smile spread across my face, and I stood on my tiptoes, placing my lips on his. *He's right. Now, go focus on your thirteen, and take out your anger productively.*

Do you want them to die? Liam winked at me and kissed me once more before turning and heading the other way.

"All right." Evan spread his arms out. "Pick a sparring partner."

"Oh, let's team-up." Max stood in front of me. "For old times' sake."

"You sure?" I wouldn't be holding anything back now.

"Yeah." He got into a fighting stance and held his fists out in front of him.

Evan made Nate fight someone else so that Bree and Sherry could team-up. When everyone got paired up, a huge smirk spread across his face. "Now, show me what you've got. Go!"

I had learned with him before; he'd make things harder on me if I didn't react, so I immediately struck out, and my hand slammed Max in the stomach.

"Holy shit." He groaned as he cradled his stomach. "I wasn't prepared."

"He said go." I circled around him, allowing my wolf to see him as prey. She would never severely hurt him, but right now, we wanted to come out on top. She wasn't going to allow us to lose like we used to.

"Fine." He straightened up and ran at me.

At the last second, I bent down, causing him to fall over me and land on his back. When he hit the ground, a loud groan left him.

"What the hell?" He rolled over on his hands and knees and jumped back onto his feet. "Where did you learn to fight this way?"

"Evan is my trainer." I held my hands up, ready to go again. As I charged him, I remembered how to throw the right punch. I punched him directly across his chin like I did the punching bag back at school, and he landed with a thud.

When he dropped to the ground, he moaned, "I'm out."

That's when it hit me that I'd learned more than I'd realized from my training. I still needed more coaching, but I wouldn't be a pushover any longer. I was a true alpha.

CHAPTER FOURTEEN

When I woke up Monday morning, I didn't immediately comprehend where I was. I glanced around the room, and the familiar silver walls and blood-red sheets told me I was in Liam's room at the academy. I still felt exhausted though. Yesterday had been a long, hard day of training, but the one bright spot was that all my work with Evan was paying off. I was getting stronger and more confident.

It had been nice to spend some time with my parents before we headed back to school, but it was hard leaving them. The council was suspicious, so in the back of my mind, I always wondered if this would be my last time to ever see them.

Liam groaned as he pulled me against his chest. *Let's pretend that your alarm clock didn't wake us up.*

That thought was way too alluring. *We're trying to stay off your dad's radar. That means we can't be late.* I turned over so I faced him and placed my lips on his. *Now, I've gotta go take a shower and try to at least look like I'm not a zombie.*

Never knew the zombie look could be such a turn-on. He deepened our kiss.

My body responded to him despite my mind's protest. It couldn't hurt to kiss for a few minutes longer.

A loud knock sounded on the door. "Get your asses up!" Evan yelled, but there was a trace of humor in his voice. "I can smell your arousal all the way out here, and we can't be late today."

It was like cold water had been dumped over me. I wasn't sure how I could face Evan after that. The longer it took to get out there, the more awkward it would be. I kissed Liam once more and pulled myself out of his hold.

"He's not the boss of us." Liam frowned as he watched me go into the closet and grab some silver tights, a black and red checkered skirt, and a red blouse with the Wolf Moon logo.

"No, he's not." I pulled out my drawer in the dresser and grabbed a bra and panties. "But he's right. I said the same thing to you before you tempted me with your body."

"And it was working, too." He winked at me. The sheet was at his waist, giving me a direct view of his chiseled abs and muscular chest. His body was so damn delicious, worthy of being licked.

He raised his hands, placing them under his head, which caused his muscles to flex even more alluringly. "I'm willing to take one for the team and piss Evan off."

My body warmed at his words, and a huge shit-eating grin filled his face. He knew I wanted to do just that, which made me even more determined to not fall for his cocky, sexy charms.

"Nah, I'm good." It took every ounce of my willpower to head into the bathroom and shut the door. Damn, I had better lock it too. Since, in all honesty, if he joined me in here, there was no chance in hell of getting out of here on time.

The door clicked as I locked it, and I heard him burst out into laughter.

"I knew you were struggling to deny me," he said the words triumphantly.

I placed my clothes on the sink and grabbed a towel from the closet. It didn't take long for me to take a cold shower and blow dry my hair. After putting my clothes and makeup on, I opened the door to find Liam dressed.

"Give me a minute to get ready, and we can head out." He walked past me into the bathroom, and I headed out toward the kitchen.

The sweet smell of pancakes and the savory smell of bacon greeted my nose as I made my way down the hallway and into the living room. When I turned into the kitchen, I found Evan filling up three plates with food on the dark granite countertop.

"Wow, what's the special occasion." I entered the kitchen and took two of the plates.

"Nothing, just struggling to sleep." His gray eyes were darker than normal as he gave me a tight smile and took his own plate to the four-seater wooden table that was open to the living room.

I sat across from Evan and put Liam's plate next to me. I was surprised to find a hot cup of coffee already brewed and waiting for me. "Everything okay?"

"Yeah..." He leaned back, looking down the hall. "No, not really."

"What's wrong?" Obviously, he didn't want Liam to overhear the conversation.

"It's Willow." He scratched the back of his neck. "I tried

talking to her when they got back the other day, but she walked past me like I didn't exist."

"Why did you want to talk to her?" I'd noticed how Evan had been watching her, but she didn't seem to return whatever attention he gave her.

"I think she's..." He took a deep breath, and his eyes locked with mine. "My mate."

"Really?" She was an arrogant hard-ass who hadn't been thrilled with our help. Could that be the reason why?

"Yeah, but I don't want anyone else to know." Evan took his fork and stabbed at the pancake. "Please."

"Your secret is safe with me." I smiled. "And she'll come around. She seems to have grown up as a rebel and hating us. It only makes sense that she isn't warming up to us."

"You're right there." Evan took a bite and chewed.

Liam's footsteps were heading in our direction, and when he saw us sitting at the table with a plate of food waiting for him, he grinned. "I'm starving."

"Well, you came to the right place." I patted the seat next to mine. "And it's delicious too." I took a huge bite and grinned. "Thank you for making it."

"One way to thank me is to not talk with your mouth full." Evan chuckled as he shook his head.

It wasn't long before we were done and Liam and I headed toward the education building.

As we reached the stairs that led up to the education building, Mr. Hale came into view.

"I see you two are heading to class," Mr. Hale pulled at his usual black suit jacket as he arched an eyebrow. His eyes flickered from Liam to me. "I'm surprised you are on time, considering how late you all got back last night."

We should've known he'd be made aware of our arrival.

The guard at the gate probably called them as soon as we had rolled in.

"We'd been hanging out and lost track of time." Liam shrugged his shoulder like it wasn't a big deal. "Did everything get straightened out? You four took off in a hurry."

"'The rebellion is getting more and more arrogant." Mr. Hale shoulder's stiffened. "We're going to have to take drastic measures and make a point. They were even brave enough to leave a symbol behind this time."

"A symbol?" We'd talked about using one, but I hadn't realized one had been made.

"Yeah, it's obvious they want to overthrow The Blood Council." He pulled out his phone and tilted it so we could see the image. It had one large ruby paw print with four smaller paw prints all the same size surrounding the larger one. "It has to be some sort of joke. Our logo doesn't have a red paw print." His face was lined with worry, but he held his head high. "Just another reason why an experienced council needs to be the one handling it."

"Are you saying you aren't handing the council over to us?" Liam was direct and stared at his father.

"Not right now, we aren't. You know it's still several months before we even need to address this." He evaded the question and took a deep breath. "I don't want to hold you two up. I'm sure I'll be seeing you soon." He smirked as he headed toward the gym building, probably meeting up with the other members.

Does he mean they aren't handing it over now because it's not your turn yet or that they don't plan on handing it over at all?

He's saying for now, but we both know they don't intend to. However, we can't react. We have to let him assume they're still in complete control. Liam took my hand and tugged me up the stairs. "Let's go."

———

WHEN I WALKED into Shifter History, I was surprised to see Professor Johnson already there. Normally, he came in at the last second and jumped into his lecture.

I paused, unsure how to proceed. "Should I wait a few minutes in the hallway?"

"No. Actually, I got here early, hoping to have a moment alone with you." The professor smiled.

Okay, I wasn't expecting that. As I made my way to my usual spot, which was the middle seat in the first row, the professor glanced around scanning the room.

"I wanted to warn you." He took several steps toward me so that we had only inches between us and lowered his voice. "That all of you heirs should be very careful. The council members are getting suspicious of you. I'd hate to lose my only living family member right after finding her."

Holy shit. He knew who I was which meant that he had to be tied to the rebellion in some sort of way. "You know?" For some reason, it meant more to me than I realized. Now that I thought about it, he was the closest to my biological dad that I'd ever get.

"Of course, I know." He ran a hand through his hair. "However, I have to be careful with my actions and words. They're always watching. You should be aware. But there is so much more going on that I haven't told anyone."

Something cold settled under my skin. "What do you mean?"

"I can't tell you here." He huffed. "I'll allow you to see it some time, but you all need to be very careful. They are putting more than guards on your trail." He forced a smile as he turned to the door as Sherry walked through it.

"Hey." She smiled at me and stopped in the doorway. "I'm sorry for interrupting."

"Come in." The professor motioned for her to come into the room. "We were catching up. That's all."

"Oh, okay." She hurried over and took her normal seat beside me.

As each student entered, they were surprised to see the professor already there. They hurried in and settled into their seats. Usually, there were multiple conversations going on, but with the professor here early, it was silent.

Moments later, Professor Johnson clapped his hands and smiled at the class. "Let's begin." He walked over to the board and wrote the word The Blood Council. "I know we've deviated from talking about the council itself, but it's time to talk about bonds."

"Like pack bonds?" The guy asked in the back.

"Yes, but also the other bonds ... Specifically the ones elite packs have." The professor nodded his head.

"Wait, you can have something other than a pack bond?" Sherry's brows furrowed.

"You can." The professor nodded. "You all are familiar with the pack bonds, but there are relationships beyond that. For instance, the council members can form a bond of mutual respect."

Yeah, I was pretty sure the current council didn't have that.

"It means that they can link to each other despite them not being each other's alpha. Back in the day with the original council, they respected each other so much that they formed a connection. Even though the Overseer is technically the strongest, he or she can't be the alpha over all;

otherwise, one region could be favored over the other. That's why the council is independent. They were able to forge a unique relationship so that in times of duress, they could speak to each other like pack members. Even though the Overseer is the strongest, the four council members could take the Overseer on if needed. For instance, if they become biased."

"What happens if one of the members of the council is the mate of the Overseer?" The question left my lips before I even processed what I'd said.

A guy in the back laughed. "There won't ever be an Overseer again, so what a stupid question."

"No, it's a good one. We are here to learn our history." Professor Johnson gave me a sad smile. "Then, that particular council member isn't allowed to sit in that seat. That would cause a conflict of interest to the Overseer regardless."

Holy shit. His words hit me right to the core.

Sherry glanced at me with concern written all over her face. We must have been thinking the same thing.

If we took over the council, Liam wouldn't be allowed to take his seat at the table. Something for which he'd trained his entire life. And what about Bree. She had never thought that she would have to lead. The information sat like a rock inside my gut.

LATER ON, we all met up at Bree and Sherry's apartment where I filled them in on everything Professor Johnson had told me prior to class starting. I'd told Liam earlier, not sure if we should tell the entire group, but he reminded me that we were all together now. It was strange for him to be the one to remind me of that.

Only, the problem was that I still didn't have the courage to tell him what I'd learned about his future. It was so damn selfish, but I wanted to handle one issue at a time. I'd promised myself I'd tell him tonight when we were alone.

Luckily, Sherry had promised me that she wouldn't tell a soul, including Simon, about what we had learned in class since it was something that Liam, Bree, and I would have to work through.

"Whoa... are we sure we should be trusting that teacher?" Micah held up one hand and shook his head. "I mean he's here for a reason."

"Yeah, so our dads can keep an eye on him." Simon glared at Micah from the corner of his eye. "That should tell you something right there."

"He's my only family member from my Dad's side." He was sincere, I could tell. "He wouldn't want me to get hurt."

"Exactly, you're emotionally tied to the man." Micah pointed at me. "Maybe we shouldn't be so trusting."

"Worst case scenario, we're more cautious." Liam shrugged. "How would that work to our detriment?"

"I agree. I think he can be trusted." Evan leaned back in his seat. "Our dads don't like him. My dad admitted that he wished he could've gotten rid of him, but after Brent died, they couldn't do anything about it. They keep him here to keep him in check. It makes sense that he'd be part of the rebellion."

"But then, why didn't they tell us?" Sherry pursed her lips.

"The less we know about what's going on here at the school, the less we can narc if we get caught." That's how they explained leaving Kai out of things. It made sense they would do the same to us.

"So, who else could be watching us?" Simon asked as he sat in the recliner, pulling Sherry on to his lap.

"Anyone. They're trying to find any reason not to hand over the council to us when the time comes. They are going to try to get as much dirt as possible on us so that they can justify it to all the packs." Liam sat on one end of the couch with me in the center next to Bree. "Any student would be willing to do it to get in their good graces."

"This complicates everything." Micah paced in front of us, a bundle of nerves. "We're going to get caught."

"If we freak out like this, then yes we will." Sherry rolled her eyes. "Everyone has to stay calm. It's not like we're going to change our minds."

"I know, but..." Micah shook his head.

"What it means is we'll need to train them at night instead of during the day." I hated to say that, but it was fact. Some of us could leave at night and have the rebellion pick us up somewhere as we stuck to the trees. "I mean, where did you get the skunk smell?" I turned my head to Liam.

"You've got to be kidding me." A small smile spread across his face.

"Okay, then cover yourself with mud." Now that I said the words out loud, maybe mud would be the better option. At least, with that, you could wash it off.

"Or we can just get Scent Killer spray." Bree stood and headed to her room.

"What is she talking about?" Simon glanced at Liam.

"Dude, I have no clue." Liam lifted both hands.

When she walked back in, she held up a huge bottle with a spray handle. "Nate gave this to me yesterday in case we needed it coming back. I hid it in my luggage. It's supposed to hide our scents completely."

"How is that possible?" Micah stopped in his tracks as he looked at the bottle.

"Apparently, humans use something like this for hunting." Bree put her nose to the sprayer. "So, Nate and his family wanted to alter it to work for wolf shifters. He said they tried it once, and it seemed promising. I guess we're about to find out."

"Do you have your phone?" Next time I saw the rebellion, I needed to get my own burner phone from them.

"Yeah, you want me to let them know our change of plans?" Bree reached behind the couch and pulled it out.

Actually, that probably wasn't a bad hiding place.

"Tell them to pick me up tonight around eleven." Evan stood and stretched. "I'll go take a nap and be ready to go. Tell them I'll meet them at the closest abandoned warehouse."

"Okay, I'll do that." Bree typed the message into her phone. "If you receive a text from me, that means don't go. No news is good news."

"Let me bag up some more clothes to take to Liam's, and we can hide the spray bottle in with them." Evan couldn't very well go outside, carrying it around. With our luck, his dad would be near and find out what it was.

"Good idea." Bree placed the bottle on the table and ran off toward her room. "Let me get your bag."

I packed a few more of my things up and grabbed my jewelry box that held my pendant. At first, I wasn't sure if staying over with Liam would work out, but I felt more comfortable with him. Now, he was my home.

After we made it back to the guys' dorms, Evan went to

take a nap, leaving me and Liam all alone. Usually, I loved moments like these, but right now, I was dreading it.

He took my hand and led me into our room. He lowered his lips to mine, and I tried kissing him back, but it felt wrong without him knowing everything. A little bit of me feared he'd reject me now, but I had to keep reminding myself that it was his decision to make; not mine.

What's going on? Liam pulled back, and his eyes turned navy blue. *You've been acting strange all afternoon.*

"I found out something today." I couldn't even get myself to use our mate bond and mind link. It felt tainted until I knew how he was going to respond. I hadn't realized how scared I was until now.

"Okay..." Unease filtered through our bond, and he took a deep breath and asked, "Does this have to do with Kai?"

"What?" I hadn't expected that reaction. "No!"

"Then what?" He lifted both hands in the air. "There is so much damn guilt rolling off you; it's scary."

"I learned something else from the professor today." I had to rip it off like a bandage even if it hurt like a bitch. "If you stay mated with me, you won't be allowed to be a member of the council."

"What?" It was as if his breath got knocked out of him. "Is this a joke?"

"No, it's not." There had to be something we could do to change this rule. "It's because the member and Overseer could be influenced by one another ... thus corrupting the purpose of the council."

"Wow." He took a step back as what I said to him processed. "So, I have to give it up or leave you?"

The fact that he even brought up leaving me hurt, but, in all fairness, I was the one who threw the option out there first. "Or I could not join the council. I mean, hell, they don't have an Overseer now."

"And look how well that's going." Liam arched an eyebrow and huffed. "All this time ... hell, and for what? Nothing." He ran his hands through his hair. "Maybe Kai had it right all along."

"What does that mean?" I wasn't sure why Kai kept being brought up in this conversation.

"He and I used to be best friends." Liam rolled his eyes and laughed even though no smile crossed his face. "We had the same tastes and interests. In fact, it's kinda funny how you played into that."

I wasn't sure how to take that comment. I was pretty sure he hadn't meant for it to be an insult, but it stung.

"Then, when I turned ten, Dad started pressuring me to learn the ways of the council. I didn't want it. I saw the life my Dad lived. He had rejected his mate; he was in a loveless marriage; he'd lost his best friend, and it was as if he was dead inside. I mean, who wants that?" He ran his hands through his hair. "While Kai got to still be a kid, I was forced to watch them beat and torture people while Kai got to go hang out at the park. I started resenting him, which made me become even more like the man I didn't want to be."

He'd gone through so much. No wonder he was an asshole when I had first met him. It broke my heart to know how young their fathers had subjected them to all of that.

"So... if you want to know the answer to your unasked question." He took a deep breath, and his eyes held something I didn't understand in them.

He was about to break my heart, and I wasn't sure if I could pick up the pieces after he did. Tears threatened my eyes, but I sucked them back. At the end of the day, I was strong, and I still had to find out what had happened to my father.

"I choose you." He dropped his hands to his sides and gave me a small smile. "Always."

It took me a second to comprehend the words. I hadn't expected them to be said. "Really?"

"Did you think I wouldn't?" He pulled me into his arms and pressed his lips to mine. "In a way, this frees me."

A sob wracked my body. "Are you sure?"

"Of course I am." He pulled me into his arms. "You had expected me to pick the council over you."

"Kind of." I wiped the tears away from my eyes but smiled. "But you do realize even if you aren't a council member, you'll be right beside me as Overseer, right?"

"'That's where I want to be." He lowered his lips to mine and kissed me so sweetly. "By your side; always."

I pulled back slightly. "You need to tell Bree." She deserved to know before the others.

"Shit, you're right." He nodded his head. "I'll tell her soon. She might not take it well though." He cringed.

The thing was that all of our lives were about to change. None of us were getting out of this unaffected.

CHAPTER FIFTEEN

The next day, after my training with Evan, Liam and I met outside the girls' dorm.

Are you sure we need to tell her? Liam frowned, and his blue eyes darkened as they met mine. He glanced at the building and back at me. His face was a mask of indifference, but the bond alerted me to his anxiety and worry.

Yes, she needs to know what her future holds. Liam had his whole life to wrap his head around being a member of the council, but Bree may have a few months at best. The longer we waited, the more off guard she would be. *She deserves the luxury of at least coming to grips with it, and she needs to be training with Evan too. She'll need to be able to hold her own.*

You're right. Liam took a deep breath and opened the main door. He waved me through as he blew out a breath. *I just want her to stay safe is all.*

This is the way you keep her safe. The truth had a way of getting out. The student area had a few girls hanging out on couches watching some stupid reality television show on the big screen.

Sometimes I wished that our group had time to do something like that. Our lives were continually focused on people being mistreated or who had been kidnapped. Maybe one day, we could have time to just be us.

Forcing all that negativity out of my mind, I took Liam's hand in mine. *And the last thing we need is for her to know we kept something like this from her.*

When we reached the dorm, I lifted my hand to knock on it when the door suddenly opened.

When I found myself face to face with Mr. Hale, I took a step back into Liam's chest.

"What are you two doing here?" Mr. Hale arched an eyebrow as anger flashed through his dark eyes. They were the same black as his suit.

"Coming by to see Bree." I forced my voice to stay level. I couldn't allow him to believe he could control me. "After all, this is my dorm too." Even though I hadn't been staying here, it was technically assigned to me.

"I'm well aware." He scowled at me.

Suddenly, it hit me. Mr. Hale, along with the other council members, always looked very young for their age, but today, Mr. Hale seemed more aged. He had faint crow's feet at the corners of his eyes, and his hair had some gray patterned in. It was very strange.

"Is something wrong?" Liam tugged me to his side. "You seem upset."

"No, I'm fine." He took a deep breath and wrinkled his nose in disgust. "I came up empty-handed, but you won't get away with it." He stared at me with such contempt before he pushed past me and headed to the elevator. "I'm on to you."

"On to me?" Could he know about the rebellion? But if so, why was he only directing his anger at me?

"I'll figure out what you're holding over them." The elevator door dinged open, and he glared at me one last time. "Enjoy yourself because your time is limited." He walked into the elevator, and the doors shut immediately.

"What the hell was that about?" It felt like I was frozen in place.

"He's acting strange." Liam opened the door and shook his head. "I've never seen him like that."

I entered the room and was surprised to not find Bree there. "Bree?"

"Mia?" Her voice sounded as if it was coming from my room.

That was odd. I walked down the hallway with Liam right on my heels, and when I turned into the room, I lost my breath at what I saw.

Drawers were scattered along the floor, the contents dumped all over, and the clothes in the closet were thrown everywhere. The only thing that remained in place were the sheets on my bed.

"What the hell happened?" Liam scanned the room.

"Dad. He came in here like a bat out of hell." Bree shrugged her shoulders. "He said something about catching her red-handed. That he was done playing games."

"What was he looking for?" Thank God I'd taken my jewelry box to Liam's ... unless he planned on going there too. *What if he's going to your place? My pendant is there.*

I'll call Evan. He should be there now. Liam pulled his phone out and dialed his friend.

"No clue." Bree shook her head. "He said he'd have the cleaners come pick up this mess, but he was scary."

"Hey, my dad may be heading over there." Liam's voice was low. "Can you go into my room and hide Mia's pendant? Also, make sure that spray is in your room." He paused a second. "Thanks, bye."

"It's like he's gone off his rocker." Bree bit her bottom lip. "Is he on to us?"

"No, I think he's trying to find out what Mia is using against us." Liam rolled his eyes.

"But I'm not..."

"I know that, but it doesn't make sense to them why the four of us are changing. He thinks there has to be a reason other than the goodness of our hearts." Liam shook his head. "It's kind of sad."

"Thank God he didn't find anything." Bree took a deep breath as she closed her eyes. "We're going to have to be more careful. I had to go run and hide the burner phone in case he came into my room. That was a close call."

Anger raged through me. "He thinks he can come in here and search my things without my permission?" This was the problem with the council. They were all entitled ass wipes.

"He was the one who paid for your first year here." Bree winced and shook her head. "This isn't right though. He was like another person."

I wondered if they felt entitled when they had killed my dad. With each passing day, I was more confident that they were the ones who did it. "Even if he paid for me to get here, he doesn't own me or my stuff."

"Oh, I agree. But they're getting desperate. They can't figure out who is on their side or not. And he wants you to get pissed and react. We can't do that." Liam shook his head with a frown. "What they don't realize is that it's most of the shifters they're supposed to be helping. But this is a good thing."

"How so?" None of this made any sense. A violation of my privacy shouldn't be considered a good thing.

"Because he knows we caught him losing control." Liam waved his hand around the room. "He's going to be embarrassed, and they are going to think twice about doing something like this again."

"Yeah, Dad doesn't like looking stupid." Bree nodded her head. "I could see that." Her forehead lined for a second, and she pursed her lips. "What are you two doing here?"

"We actually came by to tell you something." I cleared my throat and glanced at Liam. Right now, we had more important things to discuss than their father's control issues. Besides, not a damn thing was going to happen for this violation of my property. Though, one day, I'd even the score.

"Okay, what?" She examined me and pursed her lips. "Something's going on."

"Mia learned something the other day in her shifter history class." Liam started and cleared his throat.

"And..." She arched an eyebrow and bit her bottom lip.

"Long story short, you're the actual heir to the council." Liam threw the words out there so fast it was as if he thought it might make the news better.

Bree burst out laughing. "Stop messing with me. I never thought you'd joke about something like that."

"He's not joking." I touched her arm. "There is a rule that if one of the council members is the mate of the Overseer, they can't be part of the council because of that bond."

Her face dropped, and she blinked a few times. "Are you being serious?"

"Yes, I am." Liam took a deep breath as if he was preparing for the worst.

"Shit." A hand ran down her face. "No ... I can't do this."

"Yes, you can." I stepped closer to her and leaned down so I captured her attention. "You're strong. You fought for me to get here, and despite everything, you weren't willing to give up on Nate."

"Remember that one time you won against me in a fight when we were younger?" Liam winced as if it was hard for him to say. "I didn't let you win."

"What?" Bree's eyes flicked up to his. "But you told me..."

"I know what I told you, but damn, I was embarrassed." He took a deep breath. "I never fought you again after that because I didn't want it to happen again."

She ran a hand through her dark hair as she paced in front of us. "I... I wasn't trained for it."

"You were too." Liam stepped in front of her, cutting off the circle she was making. "Maybe not as hard as me, but Dad trained you, too, just in case something happened to me. You've got this."

"I guess I don't have a choice now, do I?" Her face was tight, and her body was rigid. "Then, I better up my game."

There was the strong friend I'd always known was inside her.

THE NEXT FEW weeks passed quickly. Liam was right that due to their dads' overreaction, the council was staying below the radar. They were trying to make us feel safe again, hoping I'd mess up somehow.

Mr. Hale never showed his face at Liam's dorm that day, and the heirs took news of Bree being part of the council very well... even Simon. It was surprising. However, Liam did point out that it wasn't as huge of a deal to them as it was to Bree. If something were to happen, it had always been known that she would step into his place.

Evan snuck out every night to train Bree, Sherry, and the rebels. Liam and I joined them about half the time. Liam helped train others while Bree and I were part of Evan's training group. I needed to be in the best shape possible when everything went to hell.

Micah and Simon had tried to leave with Evan once, and they almost got caught. Needless to say, Micah and Simon's missions were to be on call if we needed help distracting our fathers. Luckily, the two of them knew how to fight, so they weren't missing out on much.

Every night, our entire group had dinner together. Our group of seven had finally started to become true friends.

"Tonight, we need to focus on hand to hand combat." Evan grabbed another slice of pizza from the cardboard box that sat on the coffee table in Liam and Evan's apartment. "My wolf is on edge. The fight will be coming soon." He then leaned back in the recliner.

Their living room was set up exactly like the one in Bree's dorm room. One couch against the wall with two recliners across from one another.

"Hopefully, Micah and Simon won't need to sneak into the battle." Liam chuckled, causing his body to shake.

It tickled my right side as I took a bite sitting between him and Bree as usual.

"Oh, shut up," Simon growled as he leaned over Sherry, who was sitting on the floor in front of the other recliner, and took another slice of pizza. "It was Micah's fault that we were almost caught. He fell down at my feet."

"Whatever." Micah rolled his eyes as he sat on the floor on the other side of the coffee table, facing me. "You tripped me with your big feet."

I glanced at the clock and stood up. "We need to get ready to go. They're going to be here at eleven to get us." That was only thirty minutes from now.

"I'll go get the spray." Evan jumped to his feet and ran off to his room.

Bree stood and stretched her arms over her head. "I'm so sore. I'm not sure how I'm going to move tonight."

"You better toughen up, buttercup." Simon tilted his head in her direction. "It's only going to get rougher from here."

"Thanks, Simon, for the confidence boost." Bree narrowed her eyes at him.

"Yeah, we're working on filtering." Sherry glanced over her shoulder at her mate. "Remember, positive affirmations work best when trying to encourage someone."

"What?" His brows furrowed, and he lifted both hands. "I called her buttercup."

Micah laughed. "Calling someone a nice nickname doesn't make the rest of the sentence okay."

"Oh, leave him alone." That was the one thing I admired most about Simon even though it took me a while to realize it. He was very transparent; I knew exactly what he thought and where he stood. "He was trying to help."

"See." His eyebrows arched, and he pointed to me. "She gets me."

"Never, in a million years, did I ever think I'd hear him say that." Liam chuckled and stood, wrapping his arms around me.

"All right, spray up, everyone." Evan came out with the spray bottle.

Within minutes, we were soaked and ready to go out.

"All right, call if you need us." Sherry stood and waved Micah and Simon on. "Let's go home."

Sherry had been staying with Simon more lately as their bond solidified.

We waited a few minutes after they left and listened through the door to make sure no one was out and about. There was a party on campus, but it was in the girls' dorm, so we should be able to get to the woods without a problem from here.

"It sounds clear." Evan opened the door, and the four of us hurried to the stairwell, moving slowly to cover our noise. When we reached the back door, we ran as fast as possible to the woods that were only about twenty feet away, staying hidden there to make sure no one saw us.

Once we were confident that we hadn't drawn any attention, we began running through the woods. Evan was the leader with Bree right behind him. Liam insisted on taking up the rear.

The woods were thick, but we'd made our own trail to follow. It wasn't long before we were rushing past the girls' dorm when a guard appeared only fifty feet away from us. Evan turned around to warn us which caused Bree to stop too fast, catching her foot on a twig.

The guard's body tensed as his eyes swept in our direction.

The four of us ducked immediately, staying close to the ground.

I could only pray that he hadn't seen us in the split second it took for us to react.

We stayed perfectly still as the guard surveyed the area around him. I was able to see through a break in some leaves, and he was focused in our direction.

After about five minutes, he headed toward the guys' dorm, his eyes remaining on the woods.

Evan slowed his pace but continued on, staying close to

the ground. Once we were a good hundred yards away, we stood but moved more slowly and carefully through the woods.

After what felt like hours, we finally reached the spot of highway that we agreed to meet on. We changed our location each time in case someone noticed us one night. We were doing everything possible to keep from getting caught.

A black navigator pulled up to us, and the passenger window rolled down. Max grinned at us as he waggled his eyebrows. "Do you need a ride?"

"Really?" Kai snorted from the driver seat. "It took you the whole ride to come up with that?"

"No, I had something else, but when I saw my sister, I couldn't bring myself to say it." Max winced and frowned. "It would be borderline..."

"Stop there." I opened up the passenger back door and pointed at him. "I have a feeling it's better for everyone that way."

He bobbed his head from side to side. "Yeah, you're probably right about that."

I climbed in the very back with Liam following me while Evan and Bree sat in the middle row.

"Where's Nate?" Bree asked.

"Oh, he did a mission with Willow." Max glanced to the backseat. "He'll be back by the time we get there."

After we all got settled, I curled up in Liam's arms and took a quick nap.

As BREE and I walked toward the grassy field that served as the training area, I was surprised to find Willow heading out of a building that was used for meetings, moving in the same direction as we were.

When she looked in our direction, she frowned. "You guys are here already?"

"Yeah, we are." I forced a smile despite her negativity. "Are you joining us today?"

"Well, yeah." She sighed. "We have around four hundred now, so we need more than two trainers."

Evan appeared beside me, and his eyes scanned Willow from top to bottom. "Hey." His voice was deep and husky.

The smell of arousal hit my nose as it poured off both Willow and Evan in waves.

I hated that she was putting him through this. It was obvious she felt the same way, but something was holding her back. "How long are you going to fight this between you two?"

Bree cleared her throat and glanced at the ground.

"What are you talking about?" Willow lifted her chin.

"The mate bond." Evan was a great guy and didn't deserve this treatment. She'd been fighting it hard for two months now.

"It's never going to happen." Willow's eyes darkened as she glanced at me.

"Why not?" Evan asked as he swallowed hard.

"Because I know what you do." Willow wrinkled her nose in disgust. "My mom was Mr. Rafferty's fated mate, and he rejected her. She never recovered and died shortly after I was born. I was raised by my father, who was killed by the regional alpha because he stole food just so I could eat. I don't want anything to do with the likes of you or the council. If I had it my way, we'd still be taking the whole thing down."

Now, I understood why she was fighting it so hard.

"They're not like their fathers." Didn't she see that? Hell, they were going to fight against their fathers.

"It doesn't matter." She spat the words as she turned her back to us. "That changes nothing."

"So you're going to do the same thing to him that his dad did to your mom?" Did she not see that she was doing the exact same thing she hated the council for? "He wants you. You're the one rejecting him."

She paused in her steps as my words struck a chord with her. She glanced over her shoulder at Evan before she took a deep breath and turned away from the field, heading back to her home.

Good, maybe I finally got through to her.

I moved to follow after her when Evan caught my arm. "Don't. She needs her space," he sighed, his gray eyes darkening to metallic.

"But you're hurting." He was one of the nicest and most loyal guys I'd ever met. "I have to protect my family." The last word hung in the air.

A small smile spread across his face as he pulled me into a hug. "You're my family too." He whispered the words in my ear.

It took those words for me to finally see things for what they really were. All of these people were my family, and I'd fight like hell to save them.

CHAPTER SIXTEEN

I t was the last Friday before Christmas vacation, and we all planned on spending the next week at the rebellion camp. Time had been running at warp speed, and I was ecstatic that we'd have a normal day schedule for the next seven days. It'd been hard training at night, trying to appear awake during classes, studying, and trying to find time to sleep in between all of it.

I forced myself to stand and grabbed my backpack as I headed toward the door now that Comp One had ended.

Of course, my sexy mate leaned against the wall with a cup of coffee in each hand. He winked at me as I approached. "Here, I thought you might need this," he said as he held out one of the cups for me. "It's your favorite."

A moan left me as I held the cup to my nose and then took a sip. "Yes, I needed it desperately. Thank you." Even though I thoroughly enjoyed my next class with Professor Johnson, I was so damn tired today. "Hopefully, this will give me enough juice to last through history."

"I got an extra shot in there too." He took my hand as we

headed to the back stairwell. "After this class, go get some rest. I won't be far behind you."

Last night, we'd trained longer than normal. Although now that we had so many rebels there, we needed to increase our training. I had almost kicked Evan's ass last night, which was surprising. He told me pretty soon I'd be coaching him.

The only problem I had was my left shoulder. I'd had so many injuries to it, making it my weak spot. Evan told me ways to compensate for it when fighting, but it was my Achilles' heel if you will.

"Don't worry, I won't be stubborn this time. I need the rest." I took another sip as we walked down the stairs, enjoying the sweet taste as it rolled over my tongue.

"Good." He opened the door for me and kissed my cheek as I walked past him.

When we reached the door to my history class, I was a tad disappointed the room was empty. I'd hoped Professor Johnson would've gotten here early so he and I could have a few moments to talk again like we had been doing the past few weeks.

"Maybe something came up." Liam gave me a sad smile as his eyes met mine. "I know you were hoping he'd be here."

"Am I that obvious?"

"Well, the disappointment flowing through our bond kind of helps tip me off too." He used his free hand to grab my waist and pull me into his chest.

I stood on my tiptoes and pressed my lips against his and then pulled back. "Let me go get settled. I'll see you soon."

"Love you." He kissed my lips once more and turned, heading out the front door.

I paused, enjoying the view, and when the door shut behind him, I entered the classroom.

Once I got settled, Sherry bounced into the room. "Hey." Her eyes brightened when they met mine, and she hurried over to me to take her seat. "Everything okay?"

"Yeah, just tired," I yawned.

"Well, all right then." She chuckled. "Was it later than usual?"

"Yeah." We tried to be covert when talking out in public. You never know who might be listening.

Gertrude came into the room and frowned at me.

"Uh... hey." She'd been giving me mean looks for the past several weeks.

She rolled her eyes as she took her seat in the back.

"What's your problem?" Sherry glanced over her shoulder at the girl.

"She had to get yanked from class then Kai and Tripp go missing." Gertrude crossed her arms. "So now I'm stuck training with Barry. When I said I wanted harder training, I didn't mean hand to hand combat with a guy who's twice as strong as me."

With all the student changes going on at school, I hadn't even considered the implications that we were responsible for. "You do realize I didn't purposely do all that. It wasn't even my idea to be pulled from the class."

"Oh, I know." Her face smoothed out into one of indifference. "It's just been kinda miserable, that's all. It's easier to blame someone."

At least, she was honest.

The remaining students entered the classroom, and I glanced at the clock. Class was supposed to have begun a minute ago. The professor normally breezed through the room right when the clock turned to eleven.

I pulled out my notebook and turned to a new sheet. I grabbed my favorite teal pen and put today's date on it. The classroom buzzed with voices as we waited for our professor.

"Do you think the ten-minute rule applies here?" One guy in the back asked.

"How about the five-minute rule?" His buddy who sat beside him chuckled. "I'm ready to start break early."

"You and me both." The guy laughed.

An unsettling feeling washed over me. Something wasn't right. The professor had never been late before. Could something have happened to him? He said he was being watched closely by the council. Did they catch him doing something or worse?

"This isn't like him." Sherry glanced at the clock and back at me. "Maybe he emailed us and canceled class today." She pulled her phone from her backpack and checked her email. "No, nothing is there."

Nerves took over as I tapped my fingertips on the desk. I tried to keep my mind from running wild, but the later it got, the worse it took over. When I glanced at the clock again, it was five minutes after.

I had a feeling he wasn't coming.

"Okay, I'm out of here." The guy in the back stood and picked up his backpack, throwing it over his shoulder. "My dad is apparently coming here for a couple of days before we head home. So I better get back to my room to clean up." He made his way to the door.

That was odd. At Thanksgiving, it had been a mass exodus with no one coming on campus.

Just like with anything else, when the first stood to leave, all the others followed suit as well. It wasn't long before Sherry and I were the only ones left. We both sat there in uncomfortable silence.

"Us staying here isn't going to force him to show." She pointed at the clock that now said he was fifteen minutes late. "Come on. Let's head out."

"No, he wouldn't do something like this." I had a bad feeling deep in my gut. "Something has to be wrong."

Hey, what's going on? Liam's voice sounded in my head.

Professor Johnson. I took a deep breath, trying to get my thoughts together. *He never showed up to class.*

What? Liam even sounded surprised by that news. *My dad said his attendance and punctuality were always his strong suit. Something doesn't seem right.*

The fact that someone agreed with me didn't bring me any comfort. In fact, it made the feeling inside me grow worse. *We need to go check on him.*

Okay, give me a minute, and I'll alert the other heirs. Meet you at our dorm. His tone was intense and scared me to my core.

"Come on. We're going to Evan and Liam's dorm." I stood and threw my backpack over my shoulder as I rushed toward the door. With shaky hands, I reached into the pocket of my plaid skirt and pulled out my phone. For some reason, I hoped there was a message from the professor there. It was asinine to consider it because he didn't even have my phone number. Though at this point, I was hoping for miracles.

"Calm down." Sherry reached out to take my arm.

I dodged it, but her other hand grabbed me securely.

"You've got to calm down." She said as she jerked me around to face her before we reached the large wooden doors that led us outside. "People are watching you. If something did happen, they'd enjoy you being so upset right now." She licked her lips as she stared me right in the eyes. "You'll make mistakes if you don't get your head on straight."

Dammit. She was right, but the thought of my only family left on my dad's side being hurt affected me more than I ever thought possible. I closed my eyes and forced deep calming breaths. I wasn't sure how long I stood there like that, but when my heart rate settled, I opened my eyes. "Okay."

"Good." She opened the door with her back and waved me through. "Now, we're ready to go."

We rushed down the stairs and walked quickly across the grassy field toward the boys' dorm. As we made it through the front door, a group of guys in the corner was talking loudly, buzzing with energy.

"Yeah, the council asked for my dad to come too." One of the taller guys said as he stood proud. "He's a district alpha who now reports directly to Mr. Hale now that Mr. Thorn has been removed from his duty."

"Wow, you're lucky," One of the other ones said. "I'm just heading home, but at least we don't have any classes till next year."

"Everyone is psyched about break." Sherry rolled her eyes at me. "It'd be nice to have a home to go to."

That thought resonated with me. Yes, I'd be with my parents over the break, but it still wasn't the same thing as being home. It was strange though that some of the alphas were visiting Wolf Moon. Only, right now, there were more important matters at hand.

We rode the elevator up, and when I unlocked the door to their dorm room, I found Evan sitting on the couch, putting on his tennis shoes.

His eyes met mine, and his frown was set deep into his face. "The others should be here shortly. Then we'll go to his house and check on him."

"You know where he lives?" I don't know why, but I didn't expect that. Maybe he was in trouble and needed our help there.

"Yeah, he lives near campus so the council can keep their eye on him." He leaned over and tied his other shoe.

I entered the room and went over to the window that overlooked the grassy field. My eyes landed on Liam and Micah heading toward the dorm.

A slight knock on the door sounded a second before it opened, and Simon entered the room. He walked over to Sherry and pulled her into his arms.

"Hey, you." She said as she leaned forward and kissed his lips.

It was so nice to see the two of them so in love.

A minute later, the door opened as Micah, Liam, and Bree appeared.

"Now what's going on?" Simon asked as he pulled away from Sherry and looked at all of us.

"Professor Johnson didn't show up to class today, and we need to go check on him." It hit me how strange this was. A few months ago, none of them would've ever listened to me, but now they nodded, ready to get to business. It felt like something had snapped into place.

"We thought it might be best if all of us go to check on him." Liam made his way to me and held my waist.

"Yeah, there's no telling what's going on." Evan stood.

"Do we need to spray up?" Micah asked.

"It probably wouldn't hurt." Evan made his way down the hall. "I'll go get it."

"The rebellion hasn't heard from him either." Bree frowned as it somehow made the circles under her eyes darker. "They said he was worried yesterday that they might be on to him."

Great, it was exactly what I was afraid of.

Evan came back into the room, already soaking wet from the spray. "Here it is."

The seven of us took turns spraying each one of us down, and soon we were ready to go out the door.

"Apparently, some of the alphas are coming in to pick up their kids." It seemed odd that it would be happening right now when Professor Johnson disappeared.

"Our dads have regular meetings with the top alphas in the territories," Liam said as he put the bottle of spray on the table. "It's probably their last meeting of the year. It's nothing to be worried about."

Evan took the spray bottle and hurried back to his room. As he made his way back to us, he said, "Come on." He opened the door, and it was eerily silent. "Most of the students should be gone, but for the few who have stayed back, we'll need to be careful and keep our ears open." We hurried down the hallway, and soon we came to the last door on the left, which led us down the stairwell that had us exiting near the border of the woods.

"Stay here." Evan stepped out the door and glanced around. "Come on now." His words were just a whisper.

Our group ran into the woods deeper than normal. We all followed Evan as he ran toward the place Tripp had been kept that one day.

Today was cold even for a shifter. As we ran outside with our clothes still damp, it felt like ice cutting my skin. The chill outside closely matched the one inside me.

We kept a fast pace, and when we reached the gravel road that had led us to Tripp, Evan turned to follow it.

The ground began to descend, which helped our pace.

After about another ten minutes, Evan slowed down.

I walked beside him and saw a small house about fifty feet away. The white house looked like it had seen better days. The shingles were hanging down in several areas, and the black, wooden front door was left open. It was a one-level with some sort of shed behind it.

My heart pounded so hard it rang in my ears.

Liam stepped beside me. "It doesn't look like anyone is here."

"Yeah, but we need to be careful," Evan said as I pushed past him to make my way to the house.

"Dammit, Mia," Evan growled behind me. I heard his and Liam's footsteps both racing to catch me.

We have to plan this out. Someone could still be there. Liam caught up to me and grabbed my arm, pulling me behind a tree. *We can't lose our heads just because we're close.*

He was right. *Fine, but we need a plan. So hurry.*

"I'm going to go down there and walk around." Evan narrowed his eyes at me. "I'll be back in a second. Keep her here."

"I will." Liam pulled me against his chest as Evan moved toward the house.

Hey, it's going to be okay. Liam placed his finger under my chin, forcing me to look into his eyes. *We're going to help him.*

The others joined us a moment later.

"What's going on?" Simon leaned his head over so he could see around the tree. "Does Evan need help?"

"No, we need to stay here until he comes back." Liam glanced at the others. "Once he comes back, we'll make a plan."

An uncomfortable silence descended amongst us as we

waited. The seconds felt like minutes if not hours at this point. There was no telling what had happened to the professor or what he was going through now.

Suddenly, Evan appeared beside me, startling me enough that I had to hold back a scream.

"It looks like no one is here." Evan glanced at the place over his shoulder again. "Micah, come with me, and we'll keep an eye out behind the house."

"Good idea." Liam nodded. "Mia and I will go in and check things out. The rest of you guard the front."

"Okay." Simon nodded.

Our group slowly made our way down to the house. It was as if the house was in a little valley. When we were only about ten feet away, I turned and saw a paved road and parking space in front of the house.

I hurried in front and took one step up to the landing at the front door.

Let me go in first. Liam grabbed my hand, pulling me behind him, and stepped into the house.

The first smell that hit me when I entered was mothballs. It was so strong that I almost gagged. We made our way down a short hallway that opened to a small living room to the left and a kitchen to the right.

The cushions of the worn, black leather couch were cut open, and polyurethane foam was thrown everywhere. The old television was toppled over and broken on the ground. The walls were the same white color as outside but were dingy with dirt.

We turned toward the kitchen to find a small round table for two toppled over with two matching chairs broken on the floor. The aged, yellow-stained cabinets were wide open, and all over the grainy tile floor lay broken pieces of dishes and glass.

"Holy shit. They ransacked this place." Liam waved us down the hallway where there were three doors. The one to the right was a tiny bedroom. A full-size bed sat in the center of one wall, but the mattress was on its side as if they were searching for something under it. A small dresser sat on the other side with the drawers open, and all of the contents had been dumped on the floor.

To the left was an office that was only large enough for a desk. Just like the bedroom, the drawers had been opened, and paperwork was scattered across the floor.

Directly ahead was a bathroom that had a small toilet and stand-up shower. It seemed to be left intact.

"They were looking for something." Liam shook his head as he took it all in. "And with the amount of mess that they made, it doesn't appear that they found it."

"What do you think it was?" I glanced around, and my stomach turned when I saw a puddle of blood on the office floor. "Holy shit." I pointed in that direction.

"That's not good," he said as he frowned.

I walked into the room, and the metallic scent hit me hard. I glanced around at all the papers on the ground. As I studied them, I discovered most of them were newspaper clippings about my dad's death along with blueprints of the university buildings. "Why didn't they take all this?"

Liam's eyes followed mine. "Probably because they figure he'd already shared the information with the rebellion and it wasn't what they were looking for."

For some reason, the blood kept grabbing my attention. It looked as if he had been standing in that spot to block them from the bottom drawer. I bent down and glanced in the drawer, but it was empty. Why would he be right here instead of somewhere else?

"What are you doing?" Liam's brows furrowed as he watched me.

"He was standing here against a wall in front of this drawer." There was something here. I knew it. "He could've stood anywhere, but he was right here."

I ran my hand inside the drawer when my finger hit a raised part in the back. It was raised just enough to be able to grab. Going with instinct, I clutched the raised part of the drawer and lifted up. The wood lifted with my hand. "The bottom comes out."

"What?" He gagged from the stench of the blood. "God, that's fresh."

I couldn't focus on the scent or I wouldn't be able to figure out the secret compartment, so I pushed it from my mind. I pulled the bottom out, and Liam gasped.

"There's something on the paper." His eyes widened. "He had a hidden compartment."

I picked up the paper delicately and my breath caught in my chest when I saw what was on it. He had drawn the altar that we'd found after we got back from our trip over fall break. His rendition resembled it perfectly with the original Blood Council symbol in the center. Right next to it was written full moon.

"He was figuring out what they were using it for." That had to be what he was alluding to a few weeks ago when he told me there was something that he hadn't told anyone.

"And tonight is a full moon." Liam winced. "Do you know what that means?"

"We're going to be sneaking out and watching what happens tonight." There was no way in hell I was heading to the rebel camp tonight. We were going to find out whatever the council was trying to keep secret from everyone.

CHAPTER SEVENTEEN

L iam and I hurried out to the others. I'd placed the drawing back where the professor had hidden it because I had a feeling that was what they were searching for.

"We need to head back now." I was afraid that others may come back to search through the house again, and it was safer there than with me.

"What's wrong?" Evan asked as he and Micah hurried to the front of the house.

"We'll tell you when we get back to the dorm." Liam's words were rushed as he tugged me toward the woods. "Right now, we need to get out of here and fast."

"Okay." Bree nodded, following Liam and me as we retraced our steps.

It felt like it was taking twice as long to get back. When we were only about two miles away from the campus, I linked with Liam. *Let's tell them here so there's less of a chance of anyone overhearing.*

Okay. Liam scanned the area to make sure we were alone.

I stopped and turned to face everyone. "The house was torn apart inside."

"Torn apart how?" Evan focused on my face as if he could figure it out that way.

"They ransacked it. The cushions were sliced open, the dishes were smashed, and every drawer in the kitchen and office were dumped out.

"Do you think they found what they were looking for?" Bree took a deep breath as if preparing for my answer.

"I don't know." The image of the puddle of blood flashed into my brain. It was so vivid it was like I could smell his blood again, which made me gag. "But he was injured."

"And we found something else." Liam wrapped his strong arm around my waist and pulled me into his chest. "It was in a secret compartment in the bottom drawer of his desk."

It felt wrong to feel so safe in his arms when I knew the professor was somewhere injured.

"A secret compartment?" Micah arched an eyebrow.

"Yeah, it's hidden so no one can find it." Simon smirked.

"Not funny." Sherry side-eyed him.

"What was in it?" Evan ignored the others as he glanced from Liam back to me.

"It was a drawing of the altar we found that day." I closed my eyes, forcing that picture in my mind instead of the blood.

"With full moon written next to it." Liam mashed his lips.

"There's a full moon tonight." Evan glanced at the sky as if the moon would appear overhead.

"Then, we need to go there and watch what happens." For once, Micah seemed confident with his words.

"We need to be careful. There's no telling what or if

they found anything in the professor's house." Liam glanced around and sighed. "We need to get back and get some rest. Most of us have been up for twenty hours now."

He was right. We needed our rest or we could make stupid mistakes. "Let's go. We'll meet up at six tonight in Evan and Liam's room so we can all spray down and get over there before it gets completely dark."

"That sounds like a plan." Bree rubbed her hands together.

With our plans in place, we turned back toward the school and hurried through the woods.

Our group ran through the forest and was able to make it back into the stairwell without any problems. As we climbed the stairs, a door from the sixth floor opened.

Shit, there was no way we could all hide. We stopped in our tracks as a student and an older man stepped into the stairwell. Their skin was a paler shade, similar to Evan, and the older man was taller than what most likely was his son.

"Ah, what do we have here?" The older man pulled his gray slacks up around his waist and then grabbed his gray jacket, pulling it back down over his large belly. "The heirs and their toys?"

Great, another alpha prick to contend with.

"Why don't they smell?" His son sniffed the air as if he tried to get our scent. "That's weird."

"We were testing out a new product." It was the only thing that came to my mind. "And you proved it worked. So, thank you." I forced a smile which probably looked strange on my face. We didn't need to draw more unwanted attention to ourselves.

"Oh, neat." The younger guy took a step toward me and took another huge sniff.

A low growl emanated from Liam's chest. "Back the fuck off before I make you."

"Whoa, I thought your dad was kidding when he said you found your fated." The older man grabbed his son's arm and yanked him back. "But apparently, he wasn't."

"Look, this is a top-secret project we were working on, Mr. Kohl. One our dads want to keep secret." Evan cleared his throat and brushed past me so he was blocking me from their view. "So we don't need anyone to know, we were trying to make sure we were undetectable."

"It's because of those rebellion losers, isn't it?" The son nodded his head. "We're going to hit them so hard they won't see it coming."

His dad laughed and patted the guy on the shoulder. "I told you the council was innovative. It's nice to see we're building weapons to use against the weak. Don't let us hold you up."

My stomach dropped, but I forced my legs to continue to move up the stairs. This wasn't good. I hoped we could make it to Liam's without being caught again.

The seven of us rushed even more so, and when I saw Liam's door, my heart began to return to a normal rhythm. The seven of us rushed into the room as the distinct smell of Mr. Hale and Mr. Rafferty hit our noses.

"Did you know our dads were coming?" Liam asked as he glanced at Evan.

"No, but it's faint. They aren't here any longer." Evan shook his head. "You all go change in your rooms and hide the clothes you have on."

Liam rushed to his room, scanning everywhere as he went.

"I don't have any clothes here." Bree pointed to the door. "I'll have to go back to my room to get some."

"You can wear some of mine." I grabbed her hand and pulled her in the direction of Liam's room.

"They've been all over the place." Liam walked into his closet and grabbed a pair of jeans and a black shirt.

"Do you think they're coming back?" I rushed to the dresser and opened the bottom drawer, looking for my jewelry box I'd hidden. When I opened it up, the pendant my mother gave me was still in there.

"There's no telling." He shook his head. "I bet they were hoping we'd be gone long enough for their scents to be gone."

"Maybe." At this point, I was thinking they didn't care anymore. Something wasn't sitting right with me. The other alphas coming, Professor Johnson vanishing, and them coming into our rooms with no regard, it all appeared suspect.

I grabbed two pairs of black yoga pants and two white shirts before throwing one set at Bree. "The pants may be a little long on you, so you might need to roll them up."

"At this point, I don't care." She ran into the bathroom and arched an eyebrow. "I may be desperate to change my clothes, but I don't need to see my brother in his birthday suit."

"Don't worry. I feel the same way about you." Liam called as he went into the walk-in closet and shut the door.

A small laugh left me as I quickly changed.

"Is it safe?" Bree asked from behind the closed door.

"He's changing in the closet, so you're good." At least, this moment felt a little normal.

Both doors opened at the same time, and the three of us headed back out to the living room.

Evan was already sitting on the couch, and the others had gone.

"Nothing seemed out of place." Evan glanced in our direction. "How about in your room?"

"The same, but dad's scent was everywhere." Liam frowned.

"Even in the bathroom." Bree plopped into the recliner. "Good thing I had my phone on me."

She was referring to the burner phone the rebellion had given her, which was a very good thing. There was no telling what they'd do with that kind of information. "I wonder if they found what they were looking for."

"The spray is still where I'd left it." Evan shrugged his shoulders. "So we might not ever know."

"Yeah, right." Liam rubbed a hand down his face. "We both know they'll use it to their advantage. Whatever it is."

"Well, right now, we need to rest." We had a long night ahead of us and needed to make sure we didn't make any stupid mistakes.

"I'm going to nap out here." Evan turned and lay down on the couch long-ways.

"And if you guys don't mind, I'm going to stay here too." Bree glanced at the floor and chewed on her bottom lip. "I'm kind of afraid to be alone in my place right now."

It was sad when your best friend was afraid of her own father. "Of course, that's fine."

Even though it wasn't technically my place, Evan and Liam had never made me feel like it wasn't.

"We'll keep a lookout." Evan smiled at her as he turned on his side, facing the door.

"Sounds good to me." She grabbed the lever on the recliner and leaned the seat backward.

"Come on." Liam took my hand and guided me into the bedroom. "Let's cuddle and get some rest."

At that moment, it sounded like heaven.

A KNOCK on the bedroom door startled me from my sleep. It'd taken me awhile to finally fall asleep even wrapped in Liam's arms. I yawned as I called out, "I'm getting up." I turned and looked at the clock. It was after six, so we needed to get moving.

"Can't we just stay here?" Liam's breath hit the back of my neck with each word, making my body warm.

Now wasn't the time, no matter how much I wanted him. "I wish, but maybe one day we won't be rushing to get somewhere."

"My life has never been as hectic until I met you, but I also have never been this happy." He kissed the top of my head and released me.

"My life was pretty calm too before coming here." It was crazy to think how much had changed. I went from going to a human high school and trying to blend in to coming here, finding my mate, and learning about a life I never knew I had.

I picked up the clothes that had the scent neutralizing spray all over them and put them back on. The spray was still working, and my clothes were dry, which was a win-win for me, especially since it was going to be down below freezing tonight.

Liam hurried into the closet where he'd changed earlier and emerged with his same clothes too. He raised his arm and sniffed it. "That's so strange."

It really was. A wolf always relied on its nose, so for something to not have a scent, it was a little disorienting. "Let's go check on the others." We needed to make sure we got out there before the council. They had to be linked with the altar having the original symbol on it.

I headed to the door and opened it up. The smell of pizza hit my nose, which caused my stomach to growl.

When I walked into the living room, Bree was eating in the recliner she'd slept in, and Evan was mid-bite on the couch. Micah, Simon, and Sherry were sitting at the kitchen table with seven boxes of pizza piled in the center.

"Whoever brought this is my savior." I grabbed a paper plate next to the boxes and three pieces.

Liam was right behind me, and he joined Evan on the couch, leaving the other recliner for me.

A tense silence filled the air as we all ate. It didn't take long for all of us to finish since we were anxious and edgy. Whatever we saw tonight, there was going to be no coming back from it.

"Let me go change." Bree jumped up and went into our bathroom. I finished up my last slice right when she came back into the room.

"Let's get going. The sooner we get there, the better," Evan said as he stood and stretched.

Micah hurried to the door and placed his ear against the frame. He paused a moment and nodded his head. "There aren't any noises."

"Let's be careful. We don't need to run into anyone else this time." Liam opened the door and glanced both ways. He turned toward us and motioned us on.

My heart raced as we ran down the stairwell. With each floor we hit, more anxiety flooded me after what had happened earlier. When I reached the ground level and made it into the trees, adrenaline pumped through me.

Evan hurried to the front of the group and waved us on as we stayed within the trees. I tapped into my wolf, allowing her to take over partially. Too much stuff was running through my head, so I relied on her to get me there safely.

As we got close, the buzzing feeling under my skin took over once again like the day I had found this place. *We're getting close.*

Yeah, we are. Liam paused, allowing me to catch up with him. *What's wrong?*

That weird electric feeling is washing over me again. It was strange. It didn't hurt but didn't feel good either. It was painfully pleasant if that even made sense. How could I explain it if I didn't understand it myself?

The closer we got, the more it ran either across or under my skin. It was so intense I wasn't sure which one it was. It felt like my skin being rubbed in two different directions.

Evan slowed and pointed to a section of large trees with thick underbrush.

We're here. Liam took my hand and hunkered down as he walked along the brush to sit down far enough away so that the other five had room.

I settled beside him and looked through the greenery. We were about twenty feet away from the altar but could see everything perfectly.

Bree scooted close to me as Sherry, Simon, Micah, and then Evan filed in. I glanced at my watch and saw that it was close to a quarter after seven, so there was no telling how long we'd have to wait.

A NOISE CAME from several feet away, causing my eyes to pop open. I hadn't even realized I'd fallen asleep, but my head was on Liam's shoulder. I sat up just in time for the four council members to appear before us.

They moved slower than normal, and just like Mr. Hale, they all appeared to have aged several years in a short span of time.

"The full moon rising tonight is in our favor." Mr. Hale lifted his head toward the sky, glancing at the moon right over our heads.

It had to be close to midnight.

"Let's get this over with." Mr. Rafferty's skin seemed paler than normal as he headed to the altar and kneeled on one of the silver paw spots.

The other three followed suit, each one taking a silver paw, leaving the ruby one open.

Was my dad meant to be part of this? Was this what he was talking about when he said he needed to change something before I was brought into this world? It was hidden, and apparently, the members knew exactly what to do.

As soon as all four of them closed their eyes, the energy around me increased. The longer they stayed on the paws, the stronger it got.

What's wrong? Liam's eyes filled with concern.

Can't you feel it? It was crazy that I was the only one who seemed to be alarmed by it.

He closed his eyes as if concentrating. *I feel something, but it's not overwhelming. Almost like when we shift into our wolves.*

I hadn't even realized that. When you shift, there are a few seconds where your skin changes and sprouts fur. It was a similar feeling to that only more intense. Maybe it had something to do with that magic, but what?

Forcing myself to pay attention to what they were doing, my eyes landed back on the four members. They now had their faces lifted toward the moon. Their skin seemed to glow as the wrinkles that had just been marring their faces seemed to smooth away.

It was the most terrifying thing I'd ever experienced in my life. They were doing something unnatural, and this must explain how they always looked so young.

I glanced over to the rest of the group and noticed how Simon, Micah, and Evan rubbed their arms as if they felt the same way as I did.

Dammit, my skin feels like it's on fire. Simon's voice popped into my head, startling me. Thankfully, I was leaning against Liam so I didn't make a noise like I would've lying against a tree.

I had to be hallucinating. *Mine feels like electricity is coursing through me.*

The other three men looked directly at me.

Uh... I can hear you in my head. Micah glanced at me. *And you're not my mate.*

You're damn right about that. Liam glared at his friend.

It had to be the bond of respect that the professor taught us about in Shifter History. We were finally on the same side. Although, it didn't make sense why Liam could hear us but not Bree. She was now the official heir to the council.

"God, I feel better." Mr. Croft said as he stood and looked at the other council members.

"Not good enough." Mr. Rafferty frowned. "That rebellion has gotten out of hand."

"Don't worry. We'll take care of them just like we did Brent." A huge smirk filled Mr. Green's face.

"Let's go." Mr. Hale pointed back in the direction of the school buildings. "We have a council to maintain."

"That we do," Mr. Rafferty chuckled as he patted his friend on the shoulder.

The four of them headed back in the direction they'd come from.

We waited five minutes before standing.

Let's go. Evan motioned for us to follow him, and the seven of us hightailed it back toward the dorm room.

My thoughts were running wild. What the hell were they doing back there? And why did Bree and Sherry not feel affected like the rest of us had? None of this was making sense.

When the dorm came back into view, I took a deep breath. We had made it without being caught. At the last second, I smelled four distinct scents that shouldn't be possible.

They were dead.

"Lookie what we have here." Amber's face spread out into a huge grin as she stepped from the shadows of the forest and pulled out a gun. "Why am I not surprised?"

Evan stopped in his tracks, and Liam pulled me behind his body. Robyn and her two friends came into view to the right of us. They'd been standing at the edge of the tree line.

Turn around. Evan commanded, but as soon as we did, four guards appeared from the darkness.

None of this made sense. How had they known we'd be here?

"Mr. Hale, they're all here," Amber called out with a sick smirk on her face.

"Just as I suspected." A dark chuckle filled the night air.

There was no way out, and we'd played right into their hands.

CHAPTER EIGHTEEN

Mr. Hale's footsteps moved closer until he was standing next to Robyn. His face was smooth with none of the wrinkles I'd noticed the last time we saw each other, and the raw energy that filled the air was pouring off of him.

His face was a mask of indifference until his eyes landed on Bree. "You're in on this too?" A frown filled his face as his attention stayed locked on her.

"If you gave me more than a few minutes of your time every month, you probably would've known." She straightened her shoulders as she stared him down. "Hell, I'm the entire reason why Mia even came to this school. You knew I considered her a friend."

"Stop this emotional bullshit," Mr. Hale growled the words and turned his back to his daughter. "You've made your decision. Guards, take them to the holding place under the council building."

It made sense that they'd call it the council building since it's the very building that they conducted most of their meetings in.

"I'll make sure it gets done." Amber sneered as she stared into my eyes.

"Good." Mr. Hale nodded at her. "I'm glad I gave you four another chance." His words sounded like a proud father. "Had my son chosen you as his mate, things would've been so much better."

"All four of you are perfect to be their mates." Mr. Rafferty praised.

"Like hell they would've." Liam's words were a deep rasp.

"Let's go." A guard came up behind me and shoved us forward.

Soon, we were all heading out to the grassy knoll with ten guards at our back and their guns aimed directly at us.

There is no way out of this. Micah glanced over his shoulder and winced. *We're screwed.*

Stop whining. Simon linked to us all. *And that says something, coming from me.*

He wasn't wrong there. I glanced over my shoulder as Amber made her way over to Liam's side.

"You know, I could talk to your dad for you." She scanned his body up and down. "If you agree to drop her and be mine."

She had some nerve to not only capture us but still try to manipulate Liam. What kind of bitch does that?

"Not interested." Liam didn't even bother to glance her way.

"How does it feel to be rejected by someone even when they're held at gunpoint?" I was going to kick her ass before this was all over even if it killed me.

Bree snorted before she caught herself and reined it in. However, there was still a huge-ass grin on her face.

"You see, snakes like her only care about one thing."

Simon frowned. "Themselves. It doesn't matter that everyone else views them as pathetic, worthless, and stupid. They still want to be on top."

"Oh, shut up, Simon." Amber swung her gun in his direction. "You don't know anything about me."

"Hell if I don't." He took a deep breath and glanced at Sherry. "I was just like you until her. Thank God I woke up. To see how others viewed me makes me want to vomit."

"You've come a very long way." Sherry gave him a small smile filled with pride.

Amber scowled, which scrunched up her face, making even her beauty uglier.

The rest of the walk was spent in silence.

When we were just feet away from the doors of the building, a few of the guards moved around and got in the front while the majority stayed behind us.

The ones in front ran to the doors and opened them wide for our group to walk through.

However, I wasn't prepared for what we found.

The council was standing about twenty feet away, turned partly away from us. There were at least fifty alphas and students standing on the other side of the council.

They're here to see us being held at gunpoint. Liam's voice was full of rage, but his mask of indifference was carefully locked in place.

The guards had their guns drawn on us, making it even more of a spectacle.

Mr. Hale waved his arm in our direction. "As you can see, our own sons have turned against the council. The very one they were set to take over because of some girl." Mr. Hale pointed right at me as his nose wrinkled in disgust. "They aren't fit to lead."

Are they being serious right now? Simon's body tensed

as he stared his own dad down. "You never intended to turn it over, did you?"

"You gave us no choice." The anger in Mr. Green's amber eyes glowed. "We are doing what's best for our society."

"That's bullshit, and you know it." Simon shook his head and took a deep breath.

"Dad, come on." Micah leaned forward, trying to capture his dad's attention. "You know I've been doing everything that was asked."

"Really? Everything?" His dad's eyes flickered to his and he frowned. "You are following a nobody girl around who thinks she's more than what she is. We can't let weak-minded people take over the Blood Council."

The men behind them glared at us with disdain. They were the alphas they had brought in just for this show. I refused to cower and met each one of their stares head-on. There wasn't one single woman in the mix. It was all men... a dick party.

Stop. They wanted the heirs to beg and plead. Micah was giving them the very thing that they were hoping for. *The more you act out, the better the show. Shut it down. Now.* I lifted my chin as I took a step forward. The three guards in front immediately pointed their guns at me.

"There's no reasoning with pompous pricks that have never allowed themselves to feel something for someone other than themselves." This may be my only chance to tell these bastards how I felt. "You think you're strong, but every single one of you is half the men these heirs are. You allow your people to starve, to live in horrid conditions, to be treated as property, to be something you demean. You think you're feared, but you're not."

"Like hell we're not, you stupid, stupid girl." Mr. Rafferty charged toward me and got right in my face.

He expected me to stumble back, but I stood tall. My eyes locked on his and my wolf raised to the front. "You are hated, despised, and every single person outside of this room hopes you die a slow and miserable death."

At first, he laughed, but he must have realized that I had no intention of backing down. His smile dropped as his body shook. "That's not possible."

His breathing became rapid when he realized he wasn't going to win.

I was stronger than him even after whatever they'd just done.

Sweat appeared above his lip, and he yelled at the guards, "Get them down there now!"

You're stronger than him. Evan's shocked voice rang in my head.

One of the guards grabbed my arm, yanking me from Mr. Rafferty's gaze.

"Don't touch her," Liam pulled back his arm and punched the guard square in the face.

The guard stumbled back, letting go of my arm.

Guns pointed in Liam's direction, but it was like he was oblivious. He was staring down the guard who'd hurt me, his body tense and ready to fight again.

Stop. You're going to get hurt. I reached out and touched his arm, needing him to relax.

"See." Mr. Hale pointed at his son. "He's lost his mind over her." He shook his head in disgust. "Get him out of my sight."

The problem was we were screwed, and until we could figure something out, we needed him to keep his shit together. "Just come on." I took his hand and tugged him, making him follow me.

One of the other guards jammed a gun in Liam's back as the one he hit stood back up.

Our group continued the trek down the stairs. When we stepped into the basement, it took me by surprise. I had expected a prison, but it was a long hallway with a door on the left.

"Go on." The guard Liam had punched shoved him forward with his gun.

"I hope you remember this moment." Liam turned and looked the guard dead in the eye, "because I'll make sure that the first act of the new council will be to get retribution."

The guard laughed, but the blood dripping from the corner of his mouth made it lose some of its impact. "Yeah, you and what army? You guys will never lead us."

"Don't worry. He must have a small dick he's overcompensating for." Simon arched an eyebrow and grinned. "It has to be hard to try to overcome that."

Those comments used to irritate the hell out of me, but now that he was on our side, I found them quite funny.

Stop antagonizing them. Evan chastised him through our new link.

I'm not so thrilled about this anymore. Simon frowned as he looked at his friend.

When one of the guards opened the door, the scent of blood almost knocked me over. I forced myself to walk into the room and nearly cried with relief when I found Professor Johnson.

He was propped up on the wall with dried blood all over the side of his head and his shirt. His body seemed to sag even more when he saw me.

"Get in there." A guard outside yelled as Bree stumbled into the room.

"She was going," Micah growled as he came in behind her. "There's no reason to be a dick."

"Remember what I said..." Simon started, but Sherry cut him off. "It's not helping right now."

Simon tilted his head to the side. "You have a point."

Once Evan came through the door, the guard slammed it shut, causing it to echo through the room.

I immediately went over to the professor. "Are you okay?" I reached out to touch his head, but he pushed my hand away.

"Don't worry about me, child. You all need to worry about yourselves." He sighed as he gave me a tired smile. "I was hoping you wouldn't wind up here, but I should've known better."

"We found your drawing." I leaned over, my words barely a whisper.

"Did you watch?" His blue eyes widened.

I nodded my head. "But I'm not sure what it means."

"I have a feeling I know what it is, and it's not good." He sighed as he laid his head back on the wall.

"What do you think it is?" Liam asked as he and the others gathered around.

"It's only speculation, but it's also the only thing that makes sense." He sighed and closed his eyes. "After he left your mother that night, he stopped by my house."

"My father?" He was the only person I thought he could be referring to.

"Yes, he asked me what happens when someone uses the alpha connection to their advantage. And I told him it shouldn't be used unless absolutely needed. It would forever affect the packs." The professor opened his pain-filled eyes and mashed his lips together. "He told me his children couldn't be born into something like that."

"The alpha connection?" Micah's brows furrowed. "What is that?"

"It's something that most don't know about, but of course, the information is passed down by the council to their heirs when they take their seats at the table. During war or conflict, the top alphas can pull power from the ones underneath them in order to survive or win a war. It's to be used rarely if ever and only in extreme and desperate circumstances."

"Is that what they are doing?" Evan stared at the ground.

"I think so. It has to be." The older man leaned forward and grabbed his head. "You see, the pull has dire consequences for the pack. If done too much or to the extreme, it can cause their magic to become unhealthy. They can have health issues, their wolf is weakened, and it can cause a shifter to grow old much more quickly."

That was everything we'd seen on the tour. "Is it possible to pick who to draw it from?"

"Ah, smart girl." The professor's face filled with adoration. "Yes, they can. You see, when you lead the council, you can feel all the connections from your territory inside of you. You can feel the strongest ones down to the weakest. You can pull from many or just one."

The council pulled from the lower levels.

"How do you know all this?" Bree narrowed her eyes at him.

"Because my brother-in-law told me one night over drinks." The professor pointed at me. "He was afraid he'd have to use it since there were a few uprisings going on in the territories."

"My grandfather?" It was so weird hearing stories about my father and his family.

"Yes, apparently, if you need to use the pull, the energy kills everything the council touches during the conversion. That's what I think the altar was built for. It's cement and hard to destroy."

"This is awful." Sherry clenched her hands into fists. "They had to have done that to my dad. He got feeble in the matter of a year. They wanted that asshole to take his pack."

"Yes, they like to force alphas to rise in rank who agree with their views." The professor reached over and patted my arm. "But you five can set everything right."

"How? We're locked up in what is the equivalent to a jail cell." Micah rolled his eyes and stared at the door like he was trying to make it open with his mind.

"We need to let the rebellion know we're stuck." Bree checked her pockets like she thought her phone would magically appear. "I'm going to link with Nate and let him know."

"They should know we need help already." The professor took in a shaky breath. "I alerted them yesterday that I was afraid that the council had found out my connections. If they didn't hear from me today, that would mean I was captured."

"Bree is mated to someone back at camp. So we have something the council can't touch." Liam took my hand in his.

"Professor Johnson's right," Bree whispered as she turned toward our group. "They already knew he was captured, but now they know we all are. They're sending help."

Thank God. Maybe we could get out of this after all.

The door to the room opened, and Mr. Hale stepped

inside. "What do we have here? A family reunion." He pointed to me and then Professor Johnson. "I hate to interrupt, but I need to talk to the girl of the hour."

Holy shit. He knew about me.

Mr. Hale snapped his fingers and pointed at me. "Take her the long way upstairs and to the council room. Don't let anyone in except for the council members."

"Yes, sir." A guard entered the room with four more following behind him. As he tried to grab me, Liam pushed him aside.

One of the other guards ran over and put a gun to my head. "How about I shoot her if you don't get your ass against the wall."

Liam stopped dead in his tracks and slowly breathed as he obeyed the guard. "Here, I'm going. Don't hurt her."

"I told you she'd make you weak." Mr. Hale scoffed at him and narrowed his eyes. "But don't worry. She won't be around much longer. Hopefully, you'll turn back into a better man." He waved the guard on. "Take her upstairs immediately."

I tried to yank free, but the guard only pushed the gun into my head harder. As he pulled me out, I glanced back and saw fear in Liam's eyes. I wasn't sure what was worse. My future fate or the look of the destroyed man I loved.

CHAPTER NINETEEN

The guard grabbed a hold of my hair, fisting his hand right at my scalp as he dragged me up the stairs. Pain radiated from my skull as I stumbled, trying not to lose my footing.

"He's hurting her," Liam yelled at the top of his lungs from back in the room.

"It doesn't matter," Mr. Hale replied.

When we reached the first floor, the guard continued to drag me away from the steps and forced me toward the huge crowd of alphas who still stood there. It was like I was on parade for all of them to see.

As they marched me toward the elevator door to take me to the top floor, the alphas parted, allowing a center walkway.

It didn't take more than two steps before the insults rang in my ears.

"Look at the slut." One of the older alphas glared at me. "She must be good in bed for the heirs to follow her."

If I ever thought I'd been hurt before, I was wrong. This was the epitome of emotional and physical abuse.

"Harlot!" Another alpha spat on me as I stumbled by.

"Good for nothing woman." An alpha who was only a few years older than me growled and kicked my legs out from underneath me.

However, I wasn't able to fall to the ground since the guard had such a firm grip on my hair. At this point, I blocked out everything as I closed my eyes and reached for my connection with Liam.

What are they doing to you? Liam's voice was so low in my head it was scary.

I'm being walked through the alphas to the elevator to take me to the top floor. I wanted to cry; the tears burned my eyes, but I'd be damned if I let them have the satisfaction.

Are you fucking serious? Simon said as he linked with us, and soon, I felt Micah and Evan as well.

Yeah. I didn't have more to give them at this point. It was comforting that they were with me, but it only made me want to cry more. I had so much more to lose now than just Liam.

When we get out of here, they'll pay for everything. Liam's words were a promise in my head. *Remember their faces.*

Hell yeah, they will. Simon enunciated each word. *Those pansies will be begging for forgiveness when we're through with them.*

Don't worry. They're sending someone to get us out. Liam's words were strong in my head. *Nate just told Bree. They have to be careful though with everyone in the building.*

You guys realize when we do escape, we'll have to take down our dads, right? Micah didn't sound like he was against the idea but more like he was trying to resign himself to it.

At this point, there isn't any other option. Evan's blunt demeanor shone through.

It was one of his gifts. Cutting through all the bullshit.

I know... just making sure we are all on the same page. Micah sighed the words even in my head.

Now that we were at the elevator, the guard yanked my head, causing it to snap to the right as he pressed the UP button. Pain coursed through my neck into my spine.

A growl echoed in my head, causing Liam to sound like Simon used to—unhinged.

Just hang on. Evan's voice cracked.

Between Liam's frustration, Evan's loud voice, and all the alphas behind us yelling so loud, it was like a buzzing inside my head that I couldn't get rid of.

When the doors opened, the guard dragged me inside while four other guards surrounded me, all their guns focused on me.

The door shut, and as we began to rise, one of the guards tilted his head to the side. "How does it feel now that everyone sees you for what you truly are?"

If he thought I was going to humor him with an answer, he would be sorely disappointed.

After a second, he must have realized I wasn't going to answer because his jaw tensed. "Bitch, did you hear me?" He raised his gun and hit the butt of it against the side of my head, causing it to jerk. Pain radiated down my face, and my scalp throbbed because the other guard still held my hair at my scalp.

The world started to spin, and my stomach lurched. If I thought I'd had a headache moments ago, I was dead wrong. It felt like my head was going to implode.

Mia, are you okay? Liam's concern was clear through

our bond, but it hurt to even think let alone talk even through our link.

When the elevator opened on the top floor, the guard who grabbed me like a caveman chuckled.

I tried to dig my feet into the ground, but it was useless and only made the idiots enjoy it more. There was a chair sitting in the middle of the room, and the four council members sat behind their table with huge smiles across their faces.

They watched as the guard forced me into the chair. The guard who'd hit me with the gun tied my legs and then arms to the chair so I couldn't move. He tightened them as much as possible so the rope cut into my skin.

"That's what you get for not answering me." He sneered.

Without a second thought, I did the only thing I could. I hocked a loogie, making sure to get my blood mixed in from where he hit me, and spat it right on his face.

The sneer that had been there morphed into one of disgust and rage. He went to strike me again when Mr. Hale growled, "Stop!"

The look on the guard's face changed so rapidly from vindictive to reprimanded that it almost made me laugh. Almost.

"She's ours to discipline," Mr. Hale pointed to the door. "Now, all of you leave immediately."

Like an army of puppets, the entire group of guards headed toward the door, leaving me behind.

Just take a deep breath. Liam talked gently as if he felt my headache. *We're going to get to you soon.*

I hoped that was true. The room felt like it was spinning, and I had trouble keeping my head up.

"Well, well, well." Mr. Rafferty grinned which made

him even more terrifying. "It looks like history might repeat itself."

The fact that he was taking pleasure in that comment made me somehow hate them even more. "I'm not sure what you're talking about."

"Don't play games with us." Mr. Green's eyes were wild like Simon's used to be. "We all know who you are."

"If that's the case, why do something now?" I needed to figure out how long they'd known. There must be some sort of clue. I opened up the bond, linking with all four of the heirs. They needed to hear and see everything that their dads said.

"To be honest, we'd been curious about you for some time." Mr. Hale stood and walked around the large desk that they usually hid behind.

I guess a girl tied to a chair wasn't very threatening.

"But it was earlier today when we came across the lectures Professor Johnson had gathered for next week that we knew something must be done. He had topics circled and had a line that connected with the words great-niece." Mr. Hale blinked and glanced at the ceiling. "So that was a puzzle. He has no living relatives, or so we had thought until then. And wasn't it a coincidence that a girl was causing so much hell, one stronger than she should ever have the right to be, a student in his class."

"That doesn't prove a damn thing." That was why they searched Liam's dorm.

That's why they searched my room. Liam growled the words in my head. *They've been one step ahead the entire time.*

Try to get them to tell you as much as possible. Evan spoke quietly as if he could feel my pain.

214 JEN L. GREY

"Maybe, but then we thought another dorm search was needed." He chuckled and leaned toward me like we were good friends. "When we searched Liam's room, we stumbled upon a pendant that a girl like you shouldn't have." He held out his hands to his side. "That's a lot more than a coincidence."

"You left it there so we wouldn't be alarmed." Dammit, they were smarter than we thought.

Dammit, we should've known that. Evan's words were filled with rage.

"We couldn't have you running off to the rebellion." He paused and then tapped his finger to his lips. "Oh, let's be real. You were going to be at the rebellion headquarters regardless, but it's so much more fun to take you there personally."

"You're out of luck." Did he think I would hand the location over on a silver platter?

Do whatever it takes to stay alive. Liam's concern flowed into me. He was scared. *Tell them the location if you have to.*

I was terrified like him; however, my life wasn't worth more than so many others.

"Actually, we're not." Mr. Hale glanced at the other three council members behind him and then turned toward me with a huge smile on his face. "The girl leading the rebellion. You know, the one with the dark red hair."

Holy shit. How did he know about Willow?

This isn't good. Simon said through the link as if he needed to state the obvious.

"Well, one night she was sloppy." Mr. Hale shrugged his shoulders. "She painted that horrid new logo that you all came up with to represent the rebellion. You know the one that is like the original symbol but altered?" He arched an eyebrow as he waited for an answer.

I wasn't going to give the asshole one.

They've known their location for God knows how long. Micah sounded as if he was about ready to give up.

We've gotta get out of here. Liam's anxiety was rising, which was affecting me. *Remember you're stronger than each one of them. You're the Overseer, for fuck's sake.*

Right now, I couldn't handle his anguish, so I unlinked them all.

"Not willing to play?" Mr. Hale sighed and shrugged. "Oh, well. Anyway, one of our guards followed her back home. I must say it was nice finding such a large number of traitors in one spot."

"So what are you going to do?" They were here for a reason. "Kill me like you did my father?"

"Oh, he wasn't the one to kill him." Mr. Rafferty now stood with a cruel glint of glee. "I was. He didn't have what it takes."

"To kill someone in cold blood?" These men were monsters. "All three of the others stood by and watched you murder my father. I'm assuming you killed him over the alpha connection with the pack." I was going out on a limb, but I agreed with Professor Johnson; it was the only thing that made sense. I hated to do it, but I opened the bond back up with the other four. They needed to hear this. It wouldn't resonate with Micah as much if he didn't hear it from the source.

"How do you know about that?" Mr. Hale deflated at my words.

"It doesn't matter. You all were doing it and my dad tried to stop you." That was what happened.

"Don't make him out to be too much of a saint." Mr. Green chuckled. "In all fairness, it was his idea."

My stomach dropped. How was that possible? "Then why did you kill him?"

There's more to the story. Liam's calm voice washed over me. *Listen to it before you get upset. This may be your only chance to get answers.*

"Because it was the perfect idea." Mr. Rafferty shouted the words. "We'd even done it a few times with the full moon, and we were getting stronger and wiser. But then, he had to run into *your* mother."

"That's why we'd always told our sons to reject their fated." Mr. Croft leaned back in his seat. "We saw what happened to your father. He was the strongest of all of us with these amazing ideas and how to get there, but as soon as he claimed your mother. He changed. He was weak and not willing to do whatever it took."

They've lost their damn minds. Micah's voice sounded broken.

"Is that what you think?" My mother had grounded him. Made him see things the way they were supposed to be. "My mother made him a better leader. One that doesn't take for themselves and hurt the packs underneath."

"We don't hurt the packs." Mr. Hale jerked and pointed his finger at me. "We're strong for them. They can't live without our help. He had to die so we could reign."

"Is that how you justify it?" Rage like never before filled me. "Is that what you tell yourself so you can sleep well at night?"

"It wasn't supposed to happen like that." Mr. Hale's words sounded weak.

Your father was his best friend. Liam had told me before, but it was like he was reminding both him and me.

Don't let your guard down. Evan said the words slowly as if they were important. *They are master manipulators.*

"No, I killed him." Mr. Rafferty pounded his fist against his chest. "It was me who hid the gun and shot him when he left us no other choice. He was going to tell the packs the secret that only council members should know. He needed to be stopped."

"And you three just watched it all?" They were cowards. It was worse than what Mr. Rafferty had done. At least he had made a decision and stood by it. Those three were spectators who could've made the difference.

I'm not surprised. My father has always taught lessons physically. Evan was cold. Much like he had been the day I'd helped him after his father had hurt him during the football game.

"It doesn't matter." Mr. Hale shook his head and yelled, "Guards, load her up. We're heading to the rebellion site."

Mia, do whatever you can to not go, but make sure to stay alive. Liam's voice sounded controlled, but our bond couldn't hide his emotions. *I'm going to find you when we finally get out of here.*

There was no helping me. Even if he did, all these guards had guns. I wasn't getting out of this.

"Why are you taking me there?" Why didn't they just kill me here? Why make the effort to take me there.

"You, stupid girl, are good for only one thing." Mr. Green chuckled as his amber eyes glowed. "You're going to be a lesson for them all."

Now, I understood why Liam was freaking out.

A new set of guards came in, and within seconds, I was untied. My legs and arms screamed as the blood flowed through them once more. They forced me down the elevator, but when we reached the first floor, all of the alphas were gone.

The silence scared me more than the crude comments and hate they had spewed earlier.

They forced me to the door, and a white van was parked just outside. As I glanced at the parking lot, I saw a line of cars that were pulling out.

"What's going on?" I doubted they would answer, but the words still left my mouth.

"They're going to attack the rebellion headquarters." The guard pushed me in the shoulder, forcing me to stumble forward. "Those assholes are going down."

Holy shit. I thought it was bad enough that the council members were heading to the rebellion camp, but now all of the alphas and their kids were heading there too.

"That doesn't include the three surrounding packs who are already in position to strike." The other guard grinned, and when he glanced at me, he started laughing. "Look at her reaction. It's priceless."

"Stop fucking around. The last thing I want to do is get into trouble." Another guard said as he opened the back of the van. He climbed in and held a gun on me as I followed behind him.

The four guards sat in the back with me, and when the doors shut, the van took off.

They're taking me to the rebellion site. Some local packs are about to attack if they aren't already. Thank God we had Bree to at least warn them.

When I didn't get a response for a few seconds, I got nervous.

Mia, our football coach is getting us out. Liam's words held hope, which flooded through our bond. *The rebellion members are getting ready for the ambush. We were able to alert them before the attack. I need you to stay strong. I'm coming for you.*

The words were nice to hear, and there was a part of me that believed everything would work out. However, the problem was that a large majority of me was ready to face the same threat that had killed my father. The council wanted me dead, but I'd go down swinging even if it meant I was covered in blood.

CHAPTER TWENTY

The van was completely silent all the way to the rebellion camp. I had no clue what time it was or how long we'd been in the van. All I knew was that my head was killing me and that Liam and the others were already in their car, heading in the same direction.

We've gotten off the exit. Liam connected with me. *We'll be there in less than thirty minutes. I'm driving as fast as I can to get to you.*

Do you have any idea how far away you are from camp? Evan didn't sound like his normal calm and collected self.

Half of his concern was for me, but I also knew of another factor—Willow.

No, I'm sorry. It was taking every ounce of strength I had not to lie down and puke all over the floorboards. The knock from the gun to my head still had me reeling. Even though the world wasn't spinning as fast now, I still felt off-balance.

The van took a sharp turn, causing my injured head to hit the side. Nausea rolled through me again as my head pounded even harder. *I think we're almost there. We just took a sharp curve.*

Liam growled in frustration through our bond once more.

Bree said the first pack attacked the rebellion. Evan's words sounded relieved. *They were able to head them off though since they had warning.*

At least, we had something going on our side. *There will be more.* They were forcing more than one pack to attack.

They're ready. Simon's excitement pulsed through our bond. *We're going to kick some ass.*

I wished I held his enthusiasm, but we were heading toward my parents and brother. There was no way I could protect them. They were probably even more of a target because of me, which I hated.

The van jerked along as we hit the uneven road. I was finally able to brace myself so my head didn't keep hitting the side. I'd take being shot in the shoulder over this kind of pain.

All too soon, the van slowed down and came to a stop. I could hear doors opening and shutting from the large number of cars that had driven here.

Guys, we are here. They needed to know so Bree could alert the others.

Do whatever you can to slow them down without getting yourself hurt any worse. Liam's words were laced with so much anger.

Footsteps sounded as people headed in our direction.

The guard in front of me stared at me. "Don't get any stupid ideas."

"Don't discourage her." The greasy asshole sitting next to him laughed. "It could be entertaining."

I wouldn't allow them to get the best of me. I ignored them, focusing on the pain in my head and my upset stomach.

The back doors opened wide with Mr. Hale coming around. He turned in my direction and smiled. "It's time to show everyone who is in charge." Mr. Hale nodded at the guards. "Bring her down here, and let's head to the field. The other packs are already here and fighting.

The greasy guard grabbed my arm, making me stumble to my feet, and shoved me toward the doorway. He pushed me hard, obviously hoping I would land on my face, but I was able to keep my balance and land on my feet. It was more out of self-preservation than show.

"Stupid bitch!" He muttered as he placed his gun in the center of my back and pushed me forward.

He was the type of guy who would say he accidentally pulled the trigger, which caused my heart to pick up its pace. I tried to take deep calming breaths because I didn't need to let them know how afraid I truly was.

The sounds of fighting could be heard clearly from here. I heard growls from people in their wolf form and guns firing from others in their human form. I had a feeling it was going to be a bloody scene.

Mr. Hale walked several steps ahead of me with a bounce in each of his steps. He was obviously excited over what was about to happen. The council thought they had the upper hand.

Hell, to be real, they did at the moment. We could only hope and pray that the momentum would change in our direction.

As we stepped from the woods to the place we normally parked our cars, I could see the blood bath that had already begun. There were more rebels than the other side, but the Blood Council had more guns and better equipment.

Mr. Rafferty grabbed my arm and dragged me toward the fight.

At first, one of the rebels went to attack but stopped short when he saw me. His eyes widened, and he fell back a step.

A guard held up a rifle and shot him, which was so loud it made everyone grab their ears. People turned in our direction, their eyes landing on me.

We're close. Liam's words startled me.

I wasn't sure if he would make it in time.

"We ... want to make a message known before we continue this war." Mr. Hale glared at Mr. Rafferty as he appeared beside me and grabbed my other arm.

Great, I was in a pissing match between the two of them, which probably put me in an even more dangerous situation. Though they both were out for my demise.

"We have your beloved spy in our control as you can see." Mr. Rafferty took a few steps forward, trying to stand in front of Mr. Hale.

"What does she have to do with anything?" One of the pack members asked who had been forced to come.

"Everything." Mr. Hale hurried to stand beside me again. "We want to show you what happens to traitors."

"God, no." My mother's voice rang out loud, and I saw her hurry in my direction, tripping over her feet. "You can't."

"Oh, but we can." Mr. Green's laugh was similar to a hyena behind me.

The fact that they were hurting so many people I loved pissed me off. It was bad enough to hurt and humiliate me, but to purposely put them through hell wasn't acceptable.

"Traitors won't be tolerated." Mr. Hale lifted his chin in the air, looking at everyone down his nose.

I linked with Liam first, *I love you. More than you'll ever know*, then I linked with the group, *I'm so lucky to have met and developed a friendship with each and every one of you. I always thought we'd have more time to get to know one another, but it seems like that won't be the case.*

Don't you dare tell us goodbye. Liam's words broke even through the bond. *You're not allowed to.*

The pain radiating through the bond somehow hurt worse than my head. His heart was breaking, which added more fuel to mine.

"Take me instead of her." Mom stumbled toward us, and she fell to her knees right in front of the four council members.

"No, you'll get to live with the pain of knowing that you killed both your mate and your daughter." Mr. Rafferty's grin spread across his entire face as he took in the sight of the broken woman before him.

"She didn't kill my father. You did." I'd never felt so much hate in my entire life. These council members thrived on power and making others feel weak-- beneath them. They were the worst type of assholes out there, and somehow the heirs wound up nothing like them.

"It was all because of her." Mr. Hale glared at me; his eyes crazed. "She made him go against us. It's her fault he's dead."

"Like hell it is." Yes, I may be about to die, but that didn't mean I had to go down without a fight. "He didn't want to suck the power from the people underneath him."

"Shut your mouth, girl." Mr. Rafferty snarled as he realized I was unloading all their dirty laundry in front of the crowd.

"What?" Willow's strong words came from the area that had been the main hub of the fight. "You're fucking siphoning us?"

"She lies." Mr. Croft spoke and joined the other three. "She'd do anything in order to divide us."

That's when it hit me. "They can't siphon the rebellion because you all turned against them." That must be how they were aging faster. "It's made them weaker."

Mr. Rafferty spun around and punched me hard in the mouth, causing my neck to jerk to the left. My head hurt now in every possible direction, and I leaned over, hurling on Mr. Hale's shoes.

We'll be there in just a few seconds. Liam's voice entered my mind. *Don't give up, Mia. We're almost there.*

"What the hell?" Mr. Hale jerked back and tried kicking off the vomit that covered his shoes.

"Oh, how the mighty have fallen." Mr. Rafferty laughed.

"Why did you hit her like that if she was lying?" Max roared as he and my dad ran over. "It's pretty shitty to take advantage of someone who has been beaten to a pulp."

"Let's get this over with so we can go home." Mr. Hale grumbled and straightened his back as he faced all the shifters as the alphas began piling in beside the council members. "This is your last chance. She will pay for all your sins, but if you still choose to fight against us, you'll suffer the same fate as her."

"Now, it's time for fun." Mr. Green hurried over and placed a gun right against my temple. "Do you have any last words?"

What a stupid-ass question. "The heirs are better leaders than these assholes ever were. Support them, and take these losers down."

"Just kill her," Mr. Rafferty barked.

"My pleasure." Mr. Green's eyes focused on me.

I took a deep breath, trying not to cower in fear, and then a gunshot rang inside the clearing. I winced, waiting for the new pain, but nothing happened.

All of a sudden, the gun was removed from my head, and Mr. Green fell to the ground holding his arm.

"What the..." Mr. Hale spun around and paused. "How the hell are you six here?"

I turned to find Liam with a gun in his hand, his eyes focused solely on me.

A huge arm wrapped around my neck and pulled me back against a hard chest. The pressure around my neck continued increasing, and I gasped for breath.

"There are more ways to kill someone than a gunshot." Mr. Rafferty's chest shook with laughter as he made me his own human shield.

You're stronger than you know. Evan linked with me as he stepped beside Liam, staring me down. *Remember what I taught you.*

He was right. I was over here acting like I was defenseless. Yeah, I may have been injured, but right now, that could work in my favor. I reached up and grabbed his arm with both of my hands, releasing some of the tension on my throat as I bent my legs and pivoted, moving behind his body. Then, I lifted up, causing Mr. Rafferty to fall over my body and onto the ground.

"Holy shit." Mr. Hale's eyes widened as he took in what I'd done.

That's when chaos erupted.

Max and Dad attacked Mr. Hale as my mother stood to her feet and ran over to me.

"Are you okay?" Her eyes scanned me, and the pain of seeing my injuries was evident on her face.

I wasn't okay, but she was the one needing to be comforted. "Of course, it looks worse than it feels."

Her nose wrinkled when the putrid smell of sulfur hit her nose. "Really?"

"Okay, no. I feel like shit, but admitting it wasn't going to help anyone." I pulled her to the side and pointed at the house she'd been staying in. "Go and hide. Stay safe."

"Only if you go with me." She tugged my arms in that direction.

"She's not going anywhere." Mr. Green rushed over to me, but Liam was there in a flash. He pulled his arm back and punched the council member square in the nose. The man fell to the ground with blood pouring from both his nose and arm.

"Go fight." Mr. Croft yelled at the alphas who had followed them there. "You will be in our favor when this whole damn thing is over."

And just like puppets, the fifty or so alpha-holes ran toward the rebellion. They all deserved to get their asses kicked.

"I have to find Willow," Evan yelled as he ran through the crowd of idiots, searching for his mate.

There was no use stopping him. I could only imagine how he felt.

Liam pulled me into his arms and lowered his forehead to mine. "Do you know how damn scared I was?"

"It's not like I did it for fun." I closed my eyes, comforted by his embrace, but tears burned my eyes, and it wasn't time for me to have a meltdown. We had a council to take down. "But we have to go help them."

"Go with your mother and hide in one of the buildings." Liam pointed in that direction.

"You know I can't do that." I was the Overseer, and there was no way in hell I wouldn't be fighting with my people.

One of the older alphas and his sons raced toward me. The younger guy headed straight for Liam.

Needing to heal faster, I called my wolf forward, and my bones broke as fur grew all over my body. When I was standing on four legs, I didn't wait for the older man to get to me. I took off, charging directly for him.

I felt so much better in this form and could heal faster. Jumping, I went for his shoulder, hoping to disable him. I didn't want to kill these people. Some of this wasn't their fault. They had been trained to behave this way. Maybe, if given the chance, we could change them.

My teeth sliced into his skin, and I used them to shred the muscle. I needed to render his arm useless, but not unsalvageable.

"Ow." He yanked back as he crumpled to the ground. "You're going to pay for that."

Before he could say another word, I jumped on his chest, making his head hit the ground hard and knocking him out.

A loud howl filled the air, and soon Micah was right beside me in his wolf form as well. His dark fur nearly blended in with the night. He jumped onto someone I hadn't heard heading in my direction behind me since I was concentrating on not hurting my opponent too much.

I spun around and found him fighting his dad head-on.

His dad was still in human form, but he was connecting to his wolf enough to make his eyes glow. "Stand down, son."

The wolf shook his head no as he paced in front of me, making it clear he was protecting me.

I turned around and was relieved to find my dad taking Mom into their house. He was going to keep her safe.

That meant Max was left fighting Mr. Hale. I turned and found him fighting one-on-one with the council member, and he was beginning to lose.

I pushed my paws into the ground as I headed over to the fight.

I'll be right there. Liam's words caressed my mind. *Don't go and get hurt.*

I couldn't blame him for being so anxious. I had a tendency for getting injured.

Both Mr. Hale and Max were now in animal form. The council member charged Max and pushed him onto his back. Mr. Hale's eyes were aimed at my brother's throat.

Without waiting a second, I ran over and steamrolled Mr. Hale directly in the side, pushing him as far away from my brother as possible.

Mr. Hale spun around, making my front two paws stumble. He bared his teeth at me as he took a deep ragged breath. His eyes were filled with so much hate and disdain.

I took a moment to see how the others were faring and found Evan fighting right next to Willow in wolf form. They were taking one wolf down after another. I was happy that they were both being careful like me. Most of these wolves were being forced to fight even if they didn't want to.

We had to find a way to end this and soon. I took a deep breath, ready for another round with Mr. Hale. I didn't want to kill Liam and Bree's father. That would hurt them even if he was insane.

Just as Mr. Hale hunched down, readying himself to attack me again, a loud and sad howl filled the air. I spun around and watched as Evan collapsed to the ground with his father standing directly over him, his teeth in Evan's shoulder.

Pain filled our bond as every heir paused and looked in that direction. If this is how they felt during what I'd gone through, I hadn't realized how much of my pain they felt. One of our brothers was down, and if we didn't help him soon, he'd die.

CHAPTER TWENTY-ONE

M ax and Kai appeared beside me and attacked Mr.
Hale, giving me an opportunity to get away.

As the four of us rushed to Evan, Willow growled and launched herself onto the back of Mr. Rafferty.

The council member had to let go of his son so he could try to buck Willow off, but he wasn't able to budge her as she sunk her teeth and claws into him.

It was as if we were watching the attack in slow motion as we ran toward them; desperate to get to Evan.

Not only was this asshole responsible for killing my father, but he was trying to do the same thing to me and his own fucking son.

Without any thought, I launched myself forward, my eyes focused on his throat.

He tried to move out of the way, but Willow was still clinging to him, holding him so he couldn't dodge fast enough.

My teeth sunk into his throat. The taste and smell of copper hit me, causing my own upset stomach to heave more, but I refused to let go. I yanked my head to the side, ripping out his throat.

A gurgling sound came from Mr. Rafferty as his eyes widened and he fell to the ground.

Willow detached from the man and ran straight to Evan. She whimpered as she stood in front of her mate, protecting him.

The other packs stopped their fighting as they watched the council member dying.

He tried to stand back up as if he couldn't believe he was injured, but he stumbled to the ground hard.

Liam ran over to stand in front of me, blocking me from the view as the coppery taste washed over me, and I threw up again.

As Mr. Rafferty's breathing slowed, a glow took over his body, and an energy circled in the air.

Energy sizzled under my skin like it had at the altar, but this time, the other four heirs seemed to feel it too.

Evan lifted his head toward us as the gray in his eyes started to brighten. When I looked at the others, they were all being affected the same.

I whimpered as my animal instincts took over. It was the excess energy that Mr. Rafferty had pulled from the full moon on the altar. Since he was dying, it was escaping and flooding back into the air. I had to tell the others. *Do not try to absorb it; otherwise, the energy won't go back to its rightful owners.* My wolf knew what must be done.

I don't want it. Micah growled as it rippled across our skin as more poured from the council member's dying body.

That's a fucking understatement. Simon lowered his body to the ground. *I want it to leave now.*

As the Eastern council member took his last breath, the magic dissipated from all around us.

A loud whimper filled the air from where the other councilmen had been fighting. I turned around and found their wolves covered with gray fur. Even Micah's dad was solid white, and they all became deathly still, lying on the ground.

The ground shook for a moment as the energy appeared to seep into the ground.

Everyone stopped fighting as Mr. Thorn appeared in human form from the battlefield. His shoulders sagged as he limped by Mr. Rafferty's body and went over to the other three members. He winced as he bent down and felt their chests. After a long moment, he raised his head and stared at the masses of people. "The council members are dead."

It'd only been a few days since that horrible night that the heirs lost their fathers. It was awful in so many different ways that it was hard to comprehend. Even though their dads had treated them horribly, they had still been their blood, and each one was mourning in their own unique way.

Professor Johnson explained to us why siphoning magic from the shifters below us was so risky and was only to be done in the most dire of circumstances. The most immediate effect is that the people you are stealing from become weaker and more at risk for illnesses, but it was also addictive. He compared it to a drug. At first, you can only take it in small doses. That's why the energy had affected us so much. Somehow, over time, you build a tolerance and need more. It ruins you from the inside even if the outside seems young and fresh. The energy was shared between the four council members sort of like a circle. When Mr. Rafferty had died, it left an opening for all of the magic to escape. They'd used so much and for so long that their bodies couldn't survive without it. In the end, none of them were able to survive.

Are you ready to take your spot on the council? Liam walked out of the bathroom and into our bedroom where he wrapped his arms around me. He cupped my face with his hands, and his eyes went directly to the small bruise I still had on my head from the night I'd been held prisoner.

As ready as I'll ever be. I stood on my tiptoes and pressed my lips to his. *As long as you're by my side, I think we'll be okay.*

I can't agree with you more. He deepened my kiss, making my head dizzy. I hoped that never changed.

A loud pounding on the door interrupted us. "If I don't get sexy time, neither do you." Willow's voice burst through our moment.

"Just because your mate is injured, don't take your frustration out on us." I laughed, pulling away from Liam. "She's right, you know. We have to go prove to the alphas that we plan on taking our seats. Shake up the hierarchy." Not one alpha who had encouraged or allowed mistreatment to their pack members was going to keep his job.

It was obvious they had known it because they were trying to cause trouble. They were attempting to get the others to overthrow us. The number of people who were loyal to us had taken them by surprise. The shifters loyal to us heard what we'd done and what this new era of the council was going to look like, and no new ruling group had ever had so much damn support.

Since it was such an important occasion, we invited every one of them we could to watch our ceremony. We purposefully wore the school colors proudly because we were representing the original council and would pledge our loyalty to the founding principles that they had created.

You look damn sexy in that outfit. Liam brushed his fingertips along the low-cut, blood-red dress covering my breasts.

Oh, don't worry. Right after it's all done, we'll finish what we started. I brushed his lips once more before pulling away and heading out the door.

The four of us made our way to the hallway where Sherry, Simon, and Micah were waiting.

"Where's Bree?" Simon glanced around us as if he expected her there.

"She and Nate are meeting us out front." It was nice to say those words. Nate was perfect for Bree, and they were finally able to be a true couple where the rest of the world could see.

"All right." Simon shrugged as he headed to the elevator.

Within minutes, we were walking outside and found not only Bree and Nate but my family as well.

My mother came over and hugged me. "I'm so proud of you."

"I didn't do it by myself." I turned to the group of people around me. "Every single one of them made this happen."

"Before we get sappy, let's go." Max pulled me into a bear hug, and my dad's eyes watered as he watched.

"It's time." Mr. Thorn appeared before us, dressed in his suit, and motioned to the door. "The longer you go without claiming your rightful seats, the more volatile the bonds are."

Liam came to my side and took my hand in his as we made our way to the council building.

When we entered the huge hall, flashbacks of when I'd previously been there washed over me. There had been a group of alphas about this size, spitting at me, calling me names, and wanting to hurt me.

As I took note of who was in the room, it surprised me that a few of them actually had the nerve to show up here again. Despite that, now wasn't the time for retribution. Something more important needed to happen.

Mr. Thorn had them put up some risers so everyone could watch what was going to take place. Since I was the Overseer, I was the first to climb the steps with the other four heirs beside me.

Liam kept a firm grip on my hand as he walked out along with me. Liam was on one side and Evan was on my other. Micah stood next to Evan as Simon stayed in place next to Liam.

"We're gathered here today for the top alphas to submit to the new council. By doing so, the shifters under you will link with them as well." Mr. Thorn stepped to the side of us as he pointed at our group.

"This is a full council, which is stronger than what we have had in decades." Mr. Thorn turned toward us and gave us a nod. "Do you promise to serve and help the shifters who submit to you?"

The five of us nodded as we had been told to do and replied as one, "We do."

"Very well." He turned to address the others, but Liam cleared his throat.

"Before we ask for their acceptance of us, I have something I need to say." Liam took a deep breath and glanced out at the crowd. "Since I'm mated to Mia and I promised to serve the packs underneath, I must withdraw from my seat as a council member. My sister, Bree, is the rightful heir as I take my place beside the Overseer."

The crowd quieted at the announcement for a moment before hushed whispers could be heard.

Bree climbed the stairs, and her voice popped into my head. *I don't know what I'm doing. Maybe this was a bad idea.*

You'll be fine. I grinned. Now that Liam withdrew, she'd taken his place in the unique bond the five of us shared.

She paused for a second and glanced at me. *Holy shit, I can hear you.*

Stop cussing and take your place next to me. Simon rolled his eyes but then winked.

The crowd murmured as Bree stood tall next to Simon and took a deep breath. "I make the same oath. To listen and serve my packs."

"And unlike the council before us, we will allow our fated mates to work at our sides." This was the most important part that I believed even the original council had gotten wrong. "Our fated mates are meant to ground us and keep our hearts open." As I said the words, Sherry, Willow, and Nate joined us on the platform. Each one standing beside their mate.

"Though only the five votes will count, we will do what we think is in the best interest of those who feel as if they have no voice. We will empower and embrace each shifter who stands with us. When Micah finds his fated mate, the same expectation will be held of them." They needed to know that the voice of all would be heard and not only of the elite.

There was a moment of silence as we waited for them to submit. Half of these people were strong supporters of their parents, who would never agree to this. We weren't sure what to expect.

"I was wrong before." Kai glanced at me and then over at

Liam. "I couldn't find another group of people who could do any better." He lowered his eyes as the first to stand down. "I submit."

My brother and parents followed him, each one linking inside our chests. The rest followed suit, and before we knew it, it was time to begin our reign and right the wrongs of the ones before us.

As WE ALL headed back to our dorms, the bond between us had grown. I wasn't sure what had happened, but now the heirs and their mates were linked together in the sacred bond we shared. This was a sign that we had made the right decision.

It came with consequences and loss, but it was the road that got us pushed together. Liam grabbed my hand and muttered goodbye to the others, leading me back to our room.

As we got in the elevator heading to the twelfth floor, he pulled me into his arms. *It's time to get you out of that dress now.*

We stumbled into the dorm room and into the bedroom, our lips tangled together. As I reached to unbutton his shirt, he grabbed my hands and pulled them away.

Okay, I hadn't expected that. "What's wrong?"

"Nothing at all." He cleared his throat and took a deep breath before kneeling in front of me. "There's only one way I could think of that could be a perfect ending to today."

"What are you doing?" My heart sped up as I watched him reach inside his pocket and pull out a large oval diamond surrounded by smaller ones.

His hands shook as he held the ring out to me. "Mia Davis, will you marry me?"

Tears burned my eyes, and I shook my head yes. "Of course. Yes."

He slipped the ring on my finger and pulled me in for a long, lingering kiss.

This was proof that no matter what happened, we'd always be at each other's side.

The End

ABOUT THE AUTHOR

Jen L. Grey is a *USA Today* Bestselling Author who writes Paranormal Romance, Urban Fantasy, and Fantasy genres.

Jen lives in Tennessee with her husband, two daughters, and three miniature Australian Shepherd. Before she began writing, she was an avid reader and enjoyed being involved in the indie community. Her love for books eventually led her to writing. For more information, please visit her website and sign up for her newsletter.

Check out my future projects and book signing events at my website.
www.jenlgrey.com

ALSO BY JEN L. GREY

Wolf Moon Academy Trilogy

Shadow Mate

Blood Legacy

Rising Fate

The Royal Heir Trilogy

Wolves' Queen

Wolf Unleashed

Wolf's Claim

The Marked Wolf Trilogy

Moon Kissed

Chosen Wolf

Broken Curse

The Royal Heir Trilogy

Wolves' Queen

Wolf Unleashed

Wolf's Claim

Bloodshed Academy Trilogy

Year One

Year Two

Year Three

The Half-Breed Prison Duology (Same World As Bloodshed Academy)

Hunted

Cursed

The Artifact Reaper Series

Reaper: The Beginning

Reaper of Earth

Reaper of Wings

Reaper of Flames

Reaper of Water

Stones of Amaria (Shared World)

Kingdom of Storms

Kingdom of Shadows

Kingdom of Ruins

Kingdom of Fire

The Pearson Prophecy

Dawning Ascent

Enlightened Ascent

Reigning Ascent

Stand Alones

Death's Angel

Rising Alpha

Bloodshed Academy Trilogy

Death's Angel

Rising Alpha

Printed in Great Britain
by Amazon